WINTER
SHADOWS

Other Five Star Titles
by Will Henry:

Tumbleweeds (1999)
Ghost Wolf of Thunder Mountain (2000)
The Legend of Sotoju Mountain (2002)

WINTER
SHADOWS

A Western Duo

WILL HENRY

Five Star • Waterville, Maine

First Edition
First Printing: January 2003

Published in 2003 in conjunction with Golden West Literary Agency.

Set in 11 pt. Plantin by Elena Picard.

Printed in the United States on permanent paper.

Library of Congress Cataloging-in-Publication Data

Henry, Will, 1912–
    [Lapwai winter]
    Winter shadows : a western duo / by Will Henry.
      p. cm.
    Contents: Lapwai winter—Winter shadows
    ISBN 0-7862-3770-8 (hc : alk. paper)
    1. Joseph, Old, d. 1871—Fiction. 2. Wallowa
County (Or.)—Fiction. 3. Nez Percâ Indians—Fiction.
4. Mandan Indians—Fiction. 5. Idaho—Fiction.
6. Western stories. I. Henry, Will, 1912– Winter shadows.
II. Title.
PS3551.L393 L37 2003
813'.54—dc21   2002028430

WINTER SHADOWS

Table of Contents

Lapwai Winter   9

Winter Shadows   51

Lapwai Winter

One

I recall the day as though it were but one or two suns gone. It had been an early spring in the northeast Oregon country, the weather in mid-April being already warm and clear as late May. I was on the hillside above our village on the Wallowa River when Itsiyiyi, Coyote, the friend of my heart in those boyhood times, came racing up from the lodges below.

Poor Coyote. His eyes were wild. His nostrils were standing wide with breath. His ragged black hair was tossing like the mane of a bay pony. I pitied the little fellow. He was always so alarmed by the least affair. Now I wondered calmly what small thing brought him dashing up from the village, and I awaited his news feeling very superior in the advantage of my fourteen summers to his twelve.

But Coyote had the real news that morning. Joseph, our chief, had decided to accept the invitation of White Bird and Toohoolhoolzote to go to Montana and hunt the buffalo. Since White Bird and Toohoolhoolzote were the chiefs of the fierce White Bird and Salmon River bands—what we called the wild, or fighting, Indians as against our own more peaceful Wallowa people—no news could possibly have been more exciting to a Nez Percé boy. With a cry as high-pitched as Coyote's, I dashed off down the hill to catch up my pony and get ready.

Within the hour, the entire village was packed and our horse herd strung out on the Imnaha Trail to Idaho and the Salmon River country, where the wild bands lived. There was no trouble crossing the Snake late that afternoon, and early the following sunrise we were off up the Salmon to see the famous warrior tribes.

The prospects sent my heart soaring higher than a hawk on hunting wings. Even though my mother, who was a Christian and had gone many years to the white man's missionary school at Lapwai, talked very strongly against such "Indian nonsense" as going to the buffalo and assured me with plenty of threats that I was going to spend that coming winter at Agent Monteith's reservation school whether Joseph and my father agreed to it or not. I still could not restrain my joy at the adventure that lay ahead. I knew this was a time of times for any Nez Percé boy to remember, and I certainly was not going to let my mother's stern beliefs in her Lord Jesus, or any of her threats about the white man's school, spoil it for me. I was an Indian, and this was a time for Indians.

It was a beautiful spring day. A shower during the night had washed the sky clean as a river stone. The sun was warm and sweet. Above us on the steepening hillsides the pine jays scolded with a good will. Below us along the rushing green water of the river the redwing reedbirds whistled cheerily. Tea Kettle, my dear mouse-colored pony, tried to bite me in the leg and buck me off. Yellow Wolf, my young uncle, who was as fierce as any fighting Indian, jogged by on his traveling mare and gave me a friendly sign. Even Joseph, that strange, sad-eyed man who almost never smiled, brightened to nod and wave at me as I passed him where he sat his horse by the trail, watching and counting to

12

be sure all of his people were safely across the Snake and settled rightly upon the trail up the Salmon.

I looked all about me at that lovely pine-scented country and at my handsome, good-natured Nez Percé people riding up the sparkling river carefree and noisy-throated as the mountain birds around them, and, doing that, I thought to myself that I might well take this moment to offer up some word of thanks to Hunyewat, our Indian God. There was, too, good and real reason for the gratitude. Owing to President Grant's good treaty of the year before, the trouble between our people and the white man was over for all time. The Wallowa, our beautiful Valley of the Winding Water, had been given back to us and surely, as of that moment among the Idaho hills, there was nothing but blue sky and bird songs in the Nez Percé world.

Bobbing along on my little gray pony, I bowed my head to the morning sun and said my humble word to Hunyewat.

Indians are supposed to be very brave, even the little boys. I was not such a good Indian, I fear. When we got to White Bird Cañon where the first village of the wild bands was located, I am afraid I did great shame to my fourteen years. I certainly did not act like a boy only three summers away from his manhood.

White Bird—it was his village nestled there on the cañon floor—was not at home. Neither were his warriors. Only the old men, the women, the children were left in the silent village. Some of the old men rode out to tell us what had happened.

Word had come that the white settlers in Kamiah Valley had stopped our Nez Percé cattle herds at Kamiah Crossing of the Clearwater River. The white men had showed the Nez Percé herdsmen their rifles and told them they could not bring their cattle into the Kamiah any more. It was white man's grass now. The Indian was going to have to stay off of it. White Bird had gone that same morning to gather up Toohoolhoolzote and the Salmon River warriors to ride to the crossing. *Eeh-hahh!* Bad, very bad. There was going to be real trouble now.

The moment I heard this I knew our trip to the buffalo country was ruined. It was then that the tear came to my eye, the sniffle to my nose. Fortunately no one saw me. There were graver things to watch. Joseph's face had grown hard as the mountain rock above us.

It was a wrong thing, he told the old men, for the settlers to have closed the historic Indian road to the Kamiah grass. The Nez Percés had used that trail and those pastures since the grayest chief could remember. But it would also be a wrong thing to let White Bird and Toohoolhoolzote come up to the river ready to fight. They were dangerous Indians.

"Ollikut, Elk Water, Horse Blanket, Yellow Wolf," said Joseph quickly, "you four come with me. Go get your best horses . . . pick your buffalo racers. We must go fast."

"Where are we going?" asked Ollikut, Joseph's tall young brother.

"To Kamiah Crossing. We must stop these angry men, or there will be shooting. We have given our word against that. Do you agree?"

"Yes," said Ollikut. "We will get our horses."

In bare minutes they had mounted up and gone hammering down the trail around Buzzard Mountain to the Clearwater River. I sat there feeling my heart tear apart within me. Suddenly I saw Coyote motioning to me urgently. I guided Tea Kettle over toward him. He was on his scrubby brown colt and he had a pudgy White Bird boy with him. The boy had his own horse, a spavined paint with feet like snowshoes. I drew myself up, looking haughty.

14

"Well," I challenged Coyote, "what do you want?"

"This is Peopeo Hihhih," he replied, indicating his companion.

"Yes? What is so remarkable about that?"

"Not much. Only his father's name is Peopeo Hihhih, too."

"Coyote, what are you trying to say to me?"

"This much . . . this boy's father is Chief White Bird."

"No!"

I could not believe it. This small, ugly little animal the true son of White Bird? Impossible.

"Boy," I said, "is my friend's tongue straight? Are you the blood son of Chief White Bird?"

"No. Only the near son. My mother was his sister. But he raised me in his teepee and gave me his name. Everybody calls me Little Bird. You look like a nice boy. What's your name?"

"Heyets."

"Very fine name. It means Mountain Sheep."

"That's very smart of you, boy. And you only seven or eight summers. Imagine!"

"Seven summers." The pudgy boy smiled. "Ten more and I will be a warrior like you."

I watched him closely, but he was not bright enough to be flattering me. He actually thought I had seventeen summers. Clearly, although not clever, neither was he as stupid as I had believed. I began to feel better about my lot.

"Well," I said cheerfully, "what shall we do? Ride down the river and stone the potholes for mallard hens? Go for a swim in the Salmon? Hunt rabbits? Have a pony race?"

Instantly the fat White Bird boy was frowning at Coyote. "I thought you said he would want to go over to the

15

Clearwater and creep up on the fight at Kamiah Crossing," he said accusingly.

"I did! I did!" protested Coyote. "But with Heyets you can't tell. He changes his mind like a woman. You can't trust his mind. Neither can he."

I did not care to stand there listening to a simpleton like Coyote explaining the workings of my thoughts to a seven-year-old White Bird Indian. I grew angry.

"Be quiet!" I ordered. "Of course, I would like to go to the Clearwater and see the fight. But what is the use of such talk? It will be all over before we could get these poor crow-baits of ours halfway around the mountain." I paused, getting madder. "Coyote," I said, "from here where I now say good bye to you, I will speak no more to you in this life. I warned you. Now we are through. *Taz alago.*"

"Well, all right, good bye." Coyote shrugged. "Have it your way, Heyets. But I just thought you would like to beat Joseph and the men to Kamiah Crossing. That's why I wanted you to see Little Bird. He knows a way."

I spun Tea Kettle around. "He knows what way?" I demanded.

"The secret way of his people over the mountain, instead of around it. It's a way he says we can get our poor horses to the crossing before any of them. Before Elk Water, your father. Before Horse Blanket, Yellow Wolf's father. Before Ollikut, Joseph's brother. Before. . . ."

"Enough, enough!" I cried. "Is this true, Little Bird?"

Little Bird lifted his three small chins. "I am the son of a war chief," he said. "Would I lie to a Wallowa?"

I made as though I did not understand the insult and said: "*Eeh-hahh,* there has been too much talk. Let's go."

"Yes, that's right," spoke up Little Bird. "We have a tall mountain to get over. Follow me. And when we get up high, let your ponies have their heads. There are some places up there you will not want to look over. *Eeh-hahh!*"

Coyote and I understood that kind of instruction. We gave a happy laugh, hit our ponies with our buffalo-hide quirts, and went charging off after Little Bird's splay-footed paint. We were gone as quickly as the men before us.

That was a wild track up over the mountain, but it was a good one. We got to the Clearwater before Joseph and before even the White Bird and Salmon River warriors.

Little Bird led us off the mountain down a creekbed that had a cover of timber all the way to its joining with the river. This was below the crossing, up near which we could plainly see the white men sitting around their campfire making loud talk and boasting of the easy way they had run off Indian herders that morning.

The day was well gone now. Whippoorwills were crying on the mountain. Dusk hawks were about their bug hunting. The sun had dropped from sight beyond the western hills. Only its last shafts were striking the face of the cliffs above us. North and east, heavy clouds were coming on to rain. The river was starting to drift a chilly mist.

I shivered and suggested to my companions that we circle the white camp and go on up the river to the village of Looking Glass, the Asotin Nez Percé chief. Up there we could get a warm sleep in a dry teepee, also some good hot beef to eat for our supper.

But Little Bird had not come over the mountain to visit the Asotins, who were even more settled than the Wallowas.

"No," said the fat rascal, "I won't go up there. My father says Looking Glass is strong, but his people are weak. They take the white man's way. *Kapsis itu,* that's a bad thing."

17

"Well," I countered, "it's going to rain. We'll get soaked and lie here on the ground shaking all night. That's a bad thing, too."

"*Eeh!*" was all he could say to me. "I am a Nez Percé. You Wallowas are all women."

"Not this Wallowa!" cried Coyote. "I fear no rain. I fear no white man. I fear no fat White Bird boy. *Ki-yi-yi-yi-yi!*"

He threw back his head and burst into his yipping personal call before I could move to stop him. My stomach closed up within me like a bunching hand. Only one thing saved us from instant discovery: Coyote made such an excellent imitation of the little brush wolf for which he was named that the white men were fooled. One of them picked up his rifle and shied a shot our way. The bullet slapped through our cover at the same time my hand took Coyote across his yammering mouth. He gave a startled yelp and shut up.

The white man laughed and put down his gun and said: "By damn, I must have clipped the leetle varmint. How's thet fer luck?"

We didn't answer him, letting him think what he wanted.

It got pretty quiet.

Presently Little Bird said respectfully to me: "What I suggest, Heyets, is that we creep up the river bed and listen to the white man's talk. Coyote said your mother has been to the school at Lapwai and has taught you their language. You can tell us what they are saying up there, eh?"

I started to give them some good reason why we should not attempt this risky thing but was unfortunately spared the need. Happening to glance up the river as he spoke, my eyes grew wide.

"*Eeh,*" I whispered excitedly. "It is too late. Look up there on the cliff."

I flung out my arm, and my friends, following the point of my rigid finger to the mountainside above the white man's fire, became very still. Everything all around became very still. That was the kind of a sight it was.

On the crest of the last rise past the settler campfire, sitting their horses quietly as so many statues carved from the mountain granite, were two craggy-faced war chiefs and half a hundred unfriendly-looking eagle-feathered fighting Indians.

"*Nanitsch!*" hissed Little Bird, filling the silence with the fierce pride of his words. "Look, all you Wallowas! See who it is yonder on the hillside. It is my father, White Bird, and his friend Toohoolhoolzote, come to kill the Kamiah white men."

The fighting Indians came down the hill. They came very slow, giving us time to slip up through the river brush to be close to it all when it happened. As they rode forward, the white men left their fire and took up their rifles. They walked out on foot to meet the mounted Indians in the way such things were done. Both parties stopped about an arrow shot apart. For the Indians, White Bird and Toohoolhoolzote rode out. For the white men, it was a lanky fellow with a foxy eye and a square-built man with blunt whiskers. We knew them both. They were Narrow-Eye Chapman and Agent Monteith.

The talk began but did not go far.

Neither White Bird nor Toohoolhoolzote spoke a word of English. Monteith knew our tongue just a little, yet had to wait for Chapman to explain many things for him. Chapman was a squaw man, living with a Umatilla woman up in White Bird Cañon. The Indians knew him from a long time and took him as their friend. Still the talk kept stopping, because of Agent Monteith. Toohoolhoolzote, famous for his harsh temper, began to grow angry. He glared at the Lapwai agent, then growled angrily at Narrow-Eye Chapman.

"Curse you both," he said, "I will not stay here and listen to any more of this delaying. We know why we are here. You know why we are here. Why do we argue? I am going to ride back a way and return with my gun cocked for shooting."

"No, no," the squaw man pleaded. "Wait now, old friend, don't do that. You haven't heard the whole story yet."

Toohoolhoolzote looked at him. "Do you deny these men stopped our cattle?" he asked.

"No, I can't deny that. But. . . ."

"Never mind. I only want to know if you stopped the cattle. Now I will ask it of you one more time. Can the cattle go over the river into the Kamiah grass?"

Chapman looked around like a rabbit caught by dogs in an open meadow. Then he spoke rapidly to Agent Monteith, telling him what Toohoolhoolzote had said. The agent got very dark in the face.

"You tell that Indian," he ordered, "to bring his cattle and come to live upon the reservation as the other Nez Percés have done. Tell him there is plenty of grass at Lapwai, and be done with him. Tell him I will send for the soldiers if he does not do as I say."

But Narrow-Eye knew better than that. He shook his head. "No," he said quickly, "we can't do that. I will ask him to wait until morning with his decision. That will give us time to send back for more men. We will need every gun in the Kamiah if we stay here. We wouldn't last five minutes if they started shooting now, and they're mortal close to doing it. Those Indians are mad."

Agent Monteith peered at the angry faces of the fighting Indians, and of a sudden his own stubborn face changed. Even from as far away as our river bushes we could see him get pale above his whiskers. At once he agreed to the squaw man's plan, and Chapman turned and told the big lie to the Indians.

Toohoolhoolzote was for war right then. But White Bird looked up at the sky and said no. The light was already too far gone for good shooting. The morning would be time enough. There were only a dozen white men, and by the good light of daybreak they could be sure they got every one of them. For a moment I let out my listening breath, thinking everything was going to rest quietly at that agreement, giving Joseph time to get here and perhaps prevent the fight. I finished translating what had been said for my two friends, not thinking how they might take the white man's treachery. I had still much to learn about fighting Indians, even very small ones.

Little Bird, the moment he heard of Chapman's deceitful words to Monteith, burst from our cover like a stepped-on cottontail. Bounding through the twilight toward the Nez Percés, he kept shouting in our tongue for them to beware, to fight right then, that Narrow-Eye Chapman was sending for more guns, maybe even for the Pony Soldiers, that all of them would be killed if they waited for the morning.

When Little Bird did that—jumped and ran—I didn't know what to do, but crazy Coyote, he knew what to do. He jumped and ran after him yelling: "Wait for me! Wait for me! Wait for me!"

One of the white men, a heavy one with yellow-stained red whiskers, cursed, using his God's name, and called out to the others: "Come on, boys, we had better beat through them willows. Might be a whole litter of them red whelps in thar!"

21

With the words he leaped on his horse and plunged him into the brush where I was running around in senseless circles trying to decide which way to go. He reached down, seized me by the back of my hunting shirt, and rode back with me dangling in one great hand.

"Here, by cripes!" he bellowed. "Look it here what I found. Damn me if it ain't a leetle red swamp rat!"

Well, it was no little red swamp rat but the fourteen-year-old son of Elk Water, the Wallowa Nez Percé. Still it was no time for false pride—or anything else for that matter. Before the red-whiskered man could bring me back to the campfire and before the startled Indians could form their line to charge upon the treacherous whites, a single shot rang out upon the mountainside.

The lone bullet splashed a whining mark of lead on a big rock which stood midway of the meadow between settlers and our angry people, and a deep voice rolled down from above, saying: "Do not fight. The first man on either side to ride beyond the rock will be shot."

We all fell still, looking upward toward the cliff down which wound the Clearwater Trail.

There, fiery red in the reflected light of the disappeared sun, tall as giants on their beautiful buffalo horses, were Joseph and Ollikut, with my father and Yellow Wolf's father and Yellow Wolf himself. All save Joseph had their rifles pointed toward the midway rock, and there was still smoke curling from Ollikut's gun, showing it was he who had fired the lone shot. For himself, Joseph did not even have a gun. He was commanding the stillness with his upheld hand alone. It was a strange thing. All the Indians and all the white men likewise did his bidding. Not one man made to move himself, or his horse, or his loaded rifle in all the time it took our Wallowa chief to ride down from the cliff.

It was the first time I had seen the power of Joseph's hand. It was the first time I knew that he possessed this *wyakin*, this personal magic to command other men. I think that many of the Nez Percés had not seen it or felt it before this time, either. It was as if they did not know this Joseph, like he was a stranger among them.

The stillness hurt the ears as he made his way across the meadow toward the white men from Kamiah.

Two

Joseph talked straight with the white men. The other Indians came into the settler fire and stood at the edge of its outer light and listened without moving. But they did not talk; only Joseph talked.

In his patient way he went back to the beginning of the agreements on paper between our two peoples. He reminded Agent Monteith of the Walla Walla Peace Council of 1855 in which only the Nez Percés had stood faithfully with the white man and in which all other tribes—the Yakimas, Umatillas, Palouses, Spokanes, Coeur d'Alênes— all of them save the Nez Percés spoke against the paper and would not sign it.

Always, Joseph said, the Nez Percés had abided by that treaty. Only when the Thieves Treaty took away their lands in 1863, after gold was discovered at Oro Fino, had the Nez Percés faltered in their friendship. Even then they had made no war, only stayed apart from the white man, asking nothing but to be let alone. Now there was President Grant's good paper returning the Wallowa country to the Nez Percés. Now all should be as it was in the old friendly days. But here was the white man trying to steal the Indian's grass again. The Kamiah was Indian country. There was no treaty keeping Nez Percé cattle away from it, yet here was the white man standing at Kamiah Crossing flourishing the rifle and saying hard things to Joseph who was trying to keep the peace.

Was it not enough, cried Joseph, throwing wide his arms, that the white man had torn the gold from the Indian earth? That he had taken the best farmlands for himself? That he had built his whisky stores along the Indian trails? That he had lured the Indian children away from their parents into his Christian schools, had taught them how to pray to Jesus Christ and to sneer at the old Indian gods, had made them forget the ways of their own fathers and mothers and led them to think their own people were lower than dogs and the white man the lord of all on earth? That he had lied to, stolen from, cheated the poor trusting Nez Percés for seventy snows and more? Were not all these things enough? Did he now also have to starve the Indian as well, to stomp in his water and stale in it, too? Must he not only take what grass he needs but also that small amount necessary to the Indian's poor few cattle?

What did such a situation leave Joseph to say to White Bird and Toohoolhoolzote? What could he tell his angry brothers to keep them from fighting in the morning? If any of the white men had the answer to that question, he had better give it to Joseph now.

There was a long silence then while the white men talked it over. Then Agent Monteith showed his stumpy teeth and stood forth to talk unfriendly.

It was time, he said, for the Nez Percés to realize they could no longer move themselves and their cattle about the land as they pleased. They were going to have to keep themselves and their herds in one place from now on, even as the white men did. There was no choice. If they would not do it, the soldiers would come and make them do it.

25

Was that perfectly clear to Joseph?

Joseph was a wise man. He did not say yes, just to make a good feeling. He shook his head and said no. He did not think he understood what Agent Monteith was saying. It seemed there was possibly more intended than was stated. Would the agent try again, Joseph asked Chapman, this time with his tongue uncurled?

Chapman winced and said to Joseph: "I hope you understand that my heart is with you. I think much of my wife's people. But I am white. What can I do?"

"Do nothing," answered Joseph, "that you do not think I would do."

"Thank you, my brother," said Chapman, and went back to Monteith. The latter proved quite ready to repeat his exact meaning. He did not like Joseph because he could not fool him, so he took refuge in hard talk.

"All right." Monteith scowled. "Here is precisely what I mean . . . you and your people are not going to the buffalo any more. You are not leaving your lands to do anything. Such moving around makes the young men restless and wild. When you put your cattle out to grass and go to the buffalo, you are away six months. The children are kept out of school. They have no chance to learn the ways of the new life that will let them live side-by-side with the white man. This is a wrong thing, Joseph. We must start with the children. They must be put in school and kept there. It is the only way to real peace between our people. We must have a common God and common ways. Only through the children may this be done."

When Joseph heard this, he asked only what putting the children in school had to do with showing the rifle at Kamiah Crossing. Monteith answered him at once. Peaceful Indians, he said, were Indians who stayed in one place. Moving Indians were fighting Indians, and the day of the moving Indian was done. From this time forward the Nez Percés must do as Indian Agent John Monteith said, not as White Bird said, not as Toohoolhoolzote said, not as any other fighting chief said. And what Agent Monteith said was that the Wallowas must now stay in their level valley, the White Birds in their deep cañon, the Salmon Rivers behind their big mountain. To guarantee this obedience there was but one sure way: Put the children in the reservation school and raise them as white boys and girls. It was up to Joseph to make this clear to the other Nez Percés. Did Joseph understand?

Our chief nodded slowly. The hurt in his face would have made a stone weep. Yes, he said, for the very first time he did understand. Now it was revealed to him what the white man really wanted of the Indian. It was not to live in peace with him, as brother to brother. When the agent said that about not going to the buffalo, about the cattle not going into Kamiah, it was only an excuse. The white man knew that to shut up the Indian in a small place was to destroy his spirit, to break his heart, to kill him. If that was what Agent Monteith now wanted Joseph to tell the other chiefs, he would do it. He would tell them that either they went home and stayed there, or the Pony Soldiers would come and drive them upon the reservation. He would tell them that in any case their children must soon be sent into Lapwai School and be made to live there. But he must warn the agent that he was asking for very dangerous things.

With this low-voiced agreement, Joseph turned away from Monteith and told the fighting Indians what he had said.

I had a very good look at this last part of it. I was being held in the camp tent. The red-whiskered man was in there

27

with me, holding his bad-smelling hand across my mouth the whole time. But I could see between his fat fingers and through the slight parting of the tent flap. Of course, none of the Nez Percé knew I was in there. They all thought I had gotten away down the river and would come into their camp when I had a chance.

When Joseph told the others about not going to the buffalo any more, about the soldiers putting them on the reservation if they moved around, about Agent Monteith demanding the surrender of the children as the earnest of their good faith, the Indians did a strange thing. Their faces grew not angry but very sad, and, when Joseph had finished the last word, they turned and went back up on the mountainside without a sound. Only old Toohoolhoolzote stayed behind with Joseph, and with our Wallowa chief he now went toward the white men.

Coming up to Monteith, Joseph said: "I have told my people what you said. Now Toohoolhoolzote will tell you what my people say in return." He stood back, giving over his place to the older man. Toohoolhoolzote stared at all the white men for a moment, then nodded.

"I will be brief," he said in Nez Percé to Chapman, but fixing his gaze upon the Lapwai agent. "Tomorrow, if you are still here, there will be shooting. We are going to the buffalo. We will graze our cattle where we wish. We will not bring our children into Lapwai. Joseph is a good man, and he is your friend. Toohoolhoolzote is a bad man, and he is not your friend. When the sun comes up, remember that. *Taz alago*, Agent Monteith. Sleep light."

For a time the old man stood there, the firelight making a black spider web of the seams and dry cañons in his face skin. His mouth was set in a line as wide and ugly as a war axe cut. His eyes burned like a wolf's eyes. His expression

28

was unmoving. Suddenly I was as afraid of him as of the white men. The sight of him braced there, lean and dark and strong as a pine tree for all his sixty-eight winters, staring down all that bitter talk and all those menacing white rifles with nothing save his Nez Percé *simiakia,* his terrible Indian pride, put a chill along my spine from tail to neck bone. When he finally turned away to follow his warriors up onto the mountain, it was even quieter than when Joseph had come down the cliff trail.

Now there was only my own chief left. He told Chapman in Nez Percé that he was sad that Agent Monteith had done this dangerous thing to the spirit of the wild bands. He promised he would yet do what he could to prevent the shooting in the morning but begged Chapman to try and get the white settlers to leave the crossing when it was full dark, to be far from it when the sun came over Buzzard Mountain next day. Then he, too, turned to go.

In the last breath, however, Agent Monteith requested him to wait a moment. Wearily Joseph did so, and Monteith wheeled toward the camp tent and said: "Bates, bring that boy up here."

Red-Beard Bates grinned and spat and shoved me, stumbling, out of the tent. Outside, he pushed me forward into the fire's light to face my chief.

Joseph's tired face softened as he saw me.

But Agent Monteith's face grew hard. "Joseph," he said, "tell your people over on the mountain that I don't trust them. I will hold the boy with us until we see there is no shooting and no following us away from here. The boy will be perfectly all right. After a time you come into Lapwai, and we will talk about him. I know this boy is of your own blood, and I have an idea for him you would do well to listen to. It may be that we can use him to lead in the others. Do you understand that?"

Joseph understood it. But to Agent Monteith he merely nodded without words, while to me he spoke ever so gently in his deep voice.

"No harm will come to you, little Heyets," he said. "Go with the agent and do not fear. I shall come for you. As you wait, think well upon what you have seen here. Do you think you can remember it?"

I drew myself up. "Yes, my chief, I will always remember it."

"Good. It is a lesson about the white man that you will never learn in his school at Lapwai." He smiled, touching me softly on the shoulder. "*Taz alago,* Heyets," he said, and turned for the last time away from this dark fire by the Clearwater.

"*Taz alago,* my chief!" I called into the twilight after him, and was glad he did not look back to see the tears that stood in my eyes, no matter that I was fourteen summers and would be a warrior soon.

Three

I had never been to Lapwai longer than one day—say, as on a Sunday, to watch the tame Indians pray, or on a Saturday when they drew their agency beef and might favor a visiting wild relative with a bit of fat meat to take home at the white man's expense. Accordingly, as I now rode toward the mission school with the agent and the Kamiah settlers, I began to recover from my fright and to wonder how it might be to live on the reservation over here in Idaho for a longer while, perhaps two or three days, or even a whole week. But I did not get to find out.

We had been riding most of the night, having slipped away from the crossing as Joseph advised. Now, as the sun came up, we stopped to boil water and make coffee. Before the water started to boil in the old black pot, five Nez Percés came out of a brushy draw nearby and rode up to our fire. We knew them all. They were Joseph, Ollikut, Horse Blanket, Yellow Wolf, and Elk Water, my own father.

"Well, Joseph," demanded Agent Monteith at once, "what is this? Have you tricked me? What do you want here?"

Joseph looked at him steadily. "It is not my way to play tricks," he said. "Last night I gave you the boy so there

31

would be no trouble with those White Birds and Salmon Rivers. There was no trouble. Now I want the boy back, that is all."

"Give them the kid," I heard Narrow-Eye Chapman whisper to Monteith, but the agent set his stubborn jaw and said, no, he wouldn't do it.

Ollikut, great, handsome Ollikut, pushed his roan buffalo racer forward. He cocked his gun. "Agent," he said, "we want the boy."

"For God's sake," said Chapman out of the side of his mouth to Monteith, "give them the kid and get shut of them. What are you trying to do, get us all killed? That damned Ollikut will tackle a buzz saw bare-handed. Smarten up, you hear? These ain't agency Indians you're fooling with."

Agent Monteith stuck out his stubby beard still farther and bared his many small teeth like a cornered cave bat, but he gave in. "Joseph," he said, "I am charging you with this matter. I want this boy in school this winter. You know why. It is the only way he can learn the white man's way."

"Yes, but he should have his say what he will do."

"No, he should not. That is the trouble with you Indians. You let the children run over you. You never say no to them and you never punish them for doing wrong. Children must be taught to do as they are told."

"We teach them. But what has that got to do with striking them and saying no to everything they want? There are other ways to show them wisdom."

"Joseph, I won't argue with you. I leave it to your own mind. Whether this boy is going to grow up Indian or white is up to you. You and I are grown men. We will not change our ways. I have one God. You have another. My father taught from the Holy Book. Your father tore up the Holy

32

Book. We are as we are, you and I, but the boy can be anything that you say he can be. You are the head chief of the Wallowas, the most powerful band of the Nez Percés. If you send this boy of your own band and blood to go to school at Lapwai this winter, you will have said to all the other wild bands that you intend to take the white man's way, to obey your agent, to learn to live the new life. It will be a powerful thing for peace, an important thing for your people. What do you say? The decision is your own. You alone can make it."

It was a hard talk. I could see that Joseph was thinking much on it. I held my breath, for I was frightened again now. Of a sudden I lost all my bravery about going to Lapwai for a few days. This was serious. They were talking about the whole winter, perhaps about several winters. This could be a sad thing. I had heard many stories of boys dying at the school, of broken hearts and bad food and lonesomeness for teepee smoke and boiled cowish and dried salmon and roast elk and the smell of horse sweat and saddle leather and gun oil and powder and all of the other grand things a wild Nez Percé lad grew up with around him in his parents' lodge, his home village, and his native hunting lands.

Joseph, too, knew of these poor boys. The thought of them weighed heavily on him and made him take such a long time that Ollikut threw him a sharp glance and said: "Come on, brother, make up your mind. I feel foolish standing here with this gun cocked."

Joseph nodded to him and sighed very deeply. "All right," he said to Agent Monteith, "give us the boy now. When the grass grows brown and the smell of the first snow is like a knife in the wind, I shall bring him to you at Lapwai."

33

Four

In May, in the land of the Nez Percés, the spring sun comes first to the southern slopes of the tumbling hills that guard the wide valleys and shadowed cañons. Here in the warm sandy soil the cowish plant breaks through the mountain loam even before the snows are all gone from the rock hollows, and catch basins hold it there to water this steady rootling of the upper hills. To these cowish patches in that month of May would go my people, hungry and eager for the taste of fresh vegetables after the long winter of dried camass and smoked salmon.

The juicy roots of the cowish baked in the Nez Percé way have a bread-like, biscuity flavor, giving the plant its white man's name of biscuit-root. We called it *kouse,* and from that the settlers sometimes called us the Kouse Eaters. My people loved this fine food which was the gift of Hunyewat, and the time of its gathering was a festival time for us. All we children looked forward through the winter to the May travel to the cowish fields. Yet in May of the year that we did not go to the buffalo, I sang no gathering songs, danced no thankful dances, ate no *kouse* at the great feast held at the traditional Time of the First Eating. I sat apart and thought only of September and of the first smell of snow in the sharpening wind.

34

June was the time of going to the camass meadows. In that month my people would take up the teepees and journey happily to the upland plateaus where, in the poorly drained places, large flats of snow melt water would collect and stand. Up out of these meadow shallows, springing like green spears from the black soil beneath the water, would come the fabled blue camass plant, the lovely water hyacinth, or Indian lily of the Northwest.

Even within a few days, the surfaces of the water flats would be brightly grown as new meadow grass with its spreading leaves. Then, short weeks later, the brilliant bells of its blue blossoms would stalk out for their brief flowering. As the swift blooming passed, all the nourishment of Hunyewat's warm sky and cool snow water would go from the faded flower down into its underground bulb to store up strength and hardy life for its fortunate harvesters.

All this glad time of waiting for the camass root to become ripe and then dry for the digging, my band was camped with the other Nez Percé bands in the shady pines above the meadow. There was much gay chanting and dancing the whole while, but I did not take part in any of it. Instead, I stayed out on the mountain by myself, thinking of September and the snow wind.

Under the mellow sun of July, the shallow waters of the camass fields evaporated, the rich muck dried, and the great Indian harvest began. Now, while the men sat at their gambling games or raced their famous Appaloosa horses and while the children played at stick-and-hoop or fished and hunted the summer away, the women took out the digging tools with their stubby wooden handles and pronged elk-horn tips and pried up the ripened bulbs of the blue lily.

After that came the cooking. As many as thirty bushels of the bulbs were covered with wet meadow grass and steamed over heated stones. Then the bulbs were mashed, shaped into loaves, and sun baked into a nourishing Indian bread. This bread would keep easily six to eight moons. It was good and valuable food, having a flavor much like a sweet yam. With the flesh of the salmon and the meat of the elk, the deer, and the antelope, it fed us through the severest winter. Thus, the July camass harvest was a time of tribal joy and gratitude for the Nez Percés. But I did not join in the Thankful Sing. I only wandered afar with Tea Kettle, my small gray pony, and looked with aching loneliness out across the blue peaks, hazy cañons, lapping waters, and lofty pines of the homeland I would see no more after the grass was brown beneath the autumn wind.

In late summer, in August, after the high spring floodwater had fallen and all the rivers were running low and clear, it was the Time of Silver Waters, of the great Columbia salmon run from the sea to the headwater creeks of Nez Percé country. This was the end of the Indian year, the very highest time of thanks for my people, and the very hardest time of work for them.

When the flashing salmon came at last, the men would strain from dawn to dusk with spear and net at every leaping falls from the mighty Celilo upward to the least spawning creeklet which fed the main forks of the Salmon, Snake, Clearwater, Grande Ronde, Wallowa, and Imnaha Rivers. The sandy beaches would soon be heaped to a small child's waist with the great humpbacked fish. Then the women would work like pack horses to split, clean, rack, and smoke the bright red slabs of the blessed flesh which provided nine of every ten Nez Percé meals around the year and which kept my people from the famine that periodically visited the other Northwestern tribes.

Yes, August and the Time of Silver Waters was the real

time to offer final thanks to Hunyewat. Yet even then I could think of no gratitude, no contentment, no happiness, but only of Joseph and Agent Monteith, and after them only of the brown grass and snow smell of September and of the log-walled prison waiting for me in the school at Lapwai.

At last the Moon of Smoky Sunshine, September, was but three suns away. In that brief space it would be Sapalwit, Sunday, and Joseph would ride up to the teepee of my father and call out in his soft, deep voice: "Elk Water, where is the boy? Where is Heyets, our little Mountain Sheep? The grass is grown brown again. The skies have turned the color of gun steel. I smell snow in the wind. It is the time to keep our word to Agent Monteith."

I let two of these last three suns torture me. Then on the final night, late and when the chilling winds had blown out all the cook fire embers and no one stirred in all that peaceful camp, I crept beneath the raised rear skins of my father's teepee.

Moving like a shadow I found my faithful friend Tea Kettle where I had tethered him in a dark spruce grove that same afternoon. He whickered and rubbed me with his soft nose, and I cried a little and loved him with my arms about his bony neck. It was a bad time, but I did not think of turning back. I only climbed on his back and guided him on into the deepening timber away from the camp of my father's people there beside the salmon falls of the Kahmuenem, the Snake River, nine miles below the entrance of the Imnaha.

I was bound for the land of our mutual foes, the Shoshone. My reasoning was that, if I could take an enemy scalp, I would no longer be considered a boy. I would be a man, a warrior, fourteen summers or no, and they would no more think of sending me to school with Agent Monteith than they would my fierce uncle, Yellow Wolf.

For equipment I had Tea Kettle, that could barely come up to a lame buffalo at his best speed. I had a *kopluts,* or war club, which was no war club at all but a rabbit throwing stick cut off short to make it look like a *kopluts.* Also I had a rusted camp axe with the haft split and most of the blade broken off; a bow-and-arrow set given me by Joseph on my tenth birthday; a much-mended Pony Soldier blanket marked **US** in one corner that was stolen for me by my father from the big fort at Walla Walla; three loaves of camass bread and a side of dried salmon, and my *wyakin,* my personal war charm, a smoked baby bear's foot cured with the claws and hair left on. And, oh, yes, I had my knife naturally. No Nez Percé would think of leaving his teepee without putting on his knife. He might not put on his pants, but he would always put on his knife.

So there I was on my way to kill a Shoshone, a Snake warrior far over across the Bitterroot Mountains in the Wind River country. I might also, for good measure, while I was over there, steal a few horses. About that I had not entirely decided. It would depend on circumstances. Meanwhile, more immediate problems were developing.

I had left home in good spirit if weak flesh. Now, however, after a long time of riding through the dark forest, the balance was beginning to come even. It occurred to me, thinking about it, that I had ridden many miles. It might well be that I needed food to return my strength. Perhaps I had better stop, make a fire, roast some salmon, warm a slice of bread. When I had eaten, I would feel my old power once more. Then, although I had already ridden a great distance that night, I would go on yet farther before lying down to sleep.

I got off Tea Kettle and gathered some moss and small

sticks that I laid properly in the shelter of a wind-fallen old pine giant. With my flint I struck a tiny flame and fed it into a good little Nez Percé fire, say the size of a man's two hands spread together, and clear and clean in the manner of its burning as a pool of trout water in later autumn. I cut a green spitting stick and propped a piece of salmon and one of camass over the flames. Then I put the soldier blanket around my shoulders and leaned back against the big log to consider my journey plans. The next thing I knew, a shaft of sunlight was prying at my eyes and two very familiar Indians were crouched at my fire, eating my salmon and camass bread.

"Good morning." Chief Joseph nodded. "This is fine food, Heyets. You had better come and have some of it with us."

"Yes," said Elk Water, my father. "It is a long ride to Lapwai."

"What is the matter?" I mumbled, my mind bewildered, my eyes still spider-webbed with sleep. "What day is this? What has happened to bring you here?"

"This is Sunday," answered Joseph in his easy way. "And what has happened to bring us here is that we have come to ride with you to Agent Monteith's school. You must have left very early, Heyets. That showed a good spirit. Probably you did not wish to bother us to rise so soon. Probably it was in your heart to let us have a good morning's sleep."

"Yes," agreed my father. "Surely that was it. Heyets is a fine boy. He wanted to let us sleep. He wanted also to ride into the white man's school alone so that we would know it did not worry him, so that we would be certain his heart was strong and he was not afraid. Is that not so, Heyets?"

My eyes had grown clearer, and it was in my mind to lie

to them, to say yes, that they were right about my thoughtful actions. Yet I could not bring myself to do it. To my father I might have lied, for he was a simple man and would not have guessed the difference, no, and would not have cared a great deal for it. But Joseph—ah, Joseph was completely another matter and another man. His great, quiet face, deep, soft voice, and sad, brown eyes touched me with a faith and a feeling that would not let my tongue wander.

"No," I replied, low-voiced. "That is not the way it was at all. I was running away. I was going to the Snake country to take a Shoshone scalp so that you would think I was a man and would not send me Agent Monteith's school. My heart was like a girl's. I was weak and sore afraid. I wanted only to stay with my people, with my father and with my chief."

There was a silence then, and my father looked hard at Joseph. He turned his head away from both Joseph and me, but I could see the large swallowing bone in his throat moving up and down. Still, he did not say anything. He waited for Joseph to speak.

At last my chief raised his eyes to me and said gently: "I beg your pardon, Heyets. The wind was making such a stir in the pine trees just now that I do not believe I heard what you said. Did you hear him, Elk Water?"

"No," answered my father, "I don't think I did. What was it you said, boy?"

I looked at Elk Water, my father, and at Joseph, my chief. Then I looked beyond them up into the pine boughs above us. There was no wind moving up there, no wind at all. I shook my head, and got to my feet.

"Nothing," I said, untying Tea Kettle and kicking dirt upon my little fire. "Let us go to Lapwai and keep the word with Agent Monteith."

Five

It will not take long, now, to tell of that Lapwai winter. It was not a good thing. The memory of it turns in me like a badly knitted bone. Yet, like a badly knitted bone, it will not let me forget.

I was sick much of the time, homesick all of the time. It was a hard winter, very cold, with a lot of wet crust snow and heavy river ice the whole while. Some of my little Indian friends who sickened at the school did not grow well again. They were not watched over by Hunyewat as Heyets was. They lay down in the night and did not get up again in the morning. When we saw them, the others of us wept, even we big boys. It hurt us very much.

If they were Christian Indian children, they were buried in the churchyard. Their mothers were there; their fathers were there. All their many friends of the reservations were there to stand and say good bye to them, and to sprinkle the handful of mother earth on them as was the old custom. Agent Monteith read from the Holy Book at the graveside, and the proper songs of Jesus were sung over them. They were treated like something.

But if they were wild Indian children, like myself, their little bodies were left to lie out overnight and freeze solid like dog salmon. Then they were stacked, like so many pieces of stove wood, in the open shed behind the school-house. There they waited, all chill and white and alone, until such time as their parents could come in over the bad trails to claim them for the simple Nez Percé ceremony of the Putting to the Last Sleep.

It was not a happy or a kind place for a boy raised in the old free Indian way. It made my heart sad and lonely to stay there. In consequence and although I knew I was being watched closely because of my kinship with Joseph, both by my own and the agency people, I grew all the more determined against the Lapwai, or white man's, way.

Naturally I learned but little at the school. I already knew how to speak the white tongue from my mother. But I did not let this help me. I would not learn to write, and in reading I was like a child of but six or seven. This blind pride was my father's blood, the old Nez Percé blood, the spirit, the *simiakia* of my untamed ancestors, entering into me. I was not a wicked boy, but neither was I willing to work. I was like a young horse caught from out of a wild herd. I knew nothing but the longing to escape. The only chance to teach me anything was to first gentle me down, and there was no chance at all to gentle me down. I thought, of course, and many times, about Joseph's faith in me. I wanted to do what was right for the sake of my chief's hope that I would serve as an example to the other wild bands that they might send their children in safety, and with profit, to the white man's school at Lapwai. But my own faith was no match for my chief's. Daily I grew more troublesome to Agent Monteith. Daily he grew less certain of my salvation.

When I had been with him five moons—through the time of Christmas and into that of the New Year—it had at last become plain to Agent Monteith that I was not "settling down", as he put it, and Joseph was sent for. When my chief arrived, I was called in while the talk was made about me. Joseph began it with his usual quiet direction, getting at once to the point.

"This boy's mother," he said, "reports to me that she has visited him here at the school and you have told her that her son is a bad boy, that he will not work, and that he is as bad for the other children as for himself." He paused, looking steadily at Agent Monteith. "Now I do not remember that Heyets is a bad boy. Perhaps my memory has failed me. Since I am also of his blood, you had better tell me what you told his mother."

Agent Monteith grew angry, his usual way. "Now see here, Joseph," he blustered, "are you trying to intimidate me?"

"Excuse me, I do not understand what you mean."

"Are you trying to frighten me?"

"Never. What I want is the truth. Should that frighten you?"

"Of course not! This boy simply will not buckle down and study as he should. He will not work with the others. The class is told to draw a picture of our Lord Jesus humbly astride a lowly donkey, and this boy draws a lurid picture of an armed warrior on an Appaloosa stallion. I ask him . . . 'What picture is that, Heyets?' . . . and he says . . . 'Why, that is a picture of Yellow Wolf on Sun Eagle going to the buffalo.' Now I put it to you, Joseph, is that the right way for a boy to behave before the others? A boy upon whom we have all placed so much hope? A boy the other bands are watching to see how he fares at Lapwai? Answer me. Say what you think."

My chief frowned and pulled at his broad chin. "I don't know," he said carefully. "Does he draw well?"

"He draws extremely well, easily the best in the class."

"He draws a good horse? A proper Indian?"

"Very good. Very proper." Agent Monteith scowled. "Perfect likenesses, especially of the horse. He puts all the parts on the animal, and, when I reprimand him, he offers to take me to the Wallowa and show me that Sun Eagle is, indeed, a horse among horses." Agent Monteith blew out his fat cheeks, filling them like the gas-blown belly of a dead cow. "Now, you listen to me, Joseph! You promised to bring this boy here and make him behave himself and work hard to learn the white man's way. This has since become a serious matter for the school. It can no longer be ignored. Heyets is creating a grave discipline problem for me, I mean among the other older boys. Some of them are beginning to draw pictures of spotted Nez Percé ponies in their study Bibles. I insist to you that this is no way for this boy of your blood to carry out our bargain."

Joseph shook his head in slow sympathy. "You are right, Agent," he said, "if what you tell me is true. But before I make a decision, I would like to have you tell me one special thing Heyets has done . . . show me some example of his evil ways that I may see with my own eyes . . . so that I shall know what it is you and I are talking about." He hesitated a little, looking at the agent. "Sometimes, you know," he said, "the white brother says one thing and really means several others. It becomes difficult for an Indian to be sure."

Agent Monteith's blunt beard jutted out, but he kept his voice reasonable. "Joseph, you are the most intelligent Indian I know. You are a shrewd man by any standards, red or white. You have been to this very school yourself in the old days. You were the best pupil they ever had here before your father, Old Joseph, tore up the Bible and took you

44

away. You understand exactly what I mean and you do not have to ask me for any examples."

Joseph only nodded again and said: "Nevertheless, show me one special bad thing the boy has done."

The agent turned away quickly and picked up a study Bible from the desk of James Redwing, a Christian Wallowa boy of my own age and my best friend among the reservation Indians. He opened the book, and handed it to Joseph.

"Very well," he snapped. "Look at that!"

Joseph took the book and studied it thoughtfully. "Let us see here," he said. "Here is a picture of a young baby being carried in his mother's arms. She is riding a small mule led by her husband. They are leaving an old town of some sort in a strange land, and they are not going very fast with such a poor beast to take them. Nevertheless, they are in a great hurry. There is fear in their faces, and I believe the enemy must be pursuing them. Is there something else I have missed?"

Agent Monteith stamped his foot. "You know very well that is the Christ child fleeing Bethlehem with Mary and Joseph!"

"Oh, yes, so it is. A fine picture of all of them, too. Better than in the book they had here before."

"You know equally well," Agent Monteith continued, very cold-eyed, "what else I am talking about and what else it is you have missed. What is printed under the picture of the Christ child?"

Joseph nodded and held the book up for me to tell him the words. I did so, and he turned back to Agent Monteith and said: "The words there are 'Jesus Fleeing the Holy City'."

"Exactly. And what has some heathen pupil scrawled in by hand under that sacred title, with a Nez Percé arrow pointing to the donkey?"

My chief's face never changed. Again he held the book up to me, and again I whispered the words to him. Looking back at Agent Monteith, he shifted the Bible as though to get a better light on it and answered: "Oh, yes, there is something else, sure enough. It says . . . 'If he had used an Appaloosa pony, his enemies never would have caught up to him.' Is that what you mean?"

"That is precisely what I mean, Joseph." The agent took time to get a good breath and let some of it puff back out of his cheeks. "That added writing was done by James Redwing, a Christian Indian of your own Wallowa band and a very fine boy who, until these past months, has been our star pupil. James is fifteen years old and I have worked with him a long time, Joseph. He had become a white boy in his thoughts and in his actions. I had saved him. He prayed on his knees every day, and he had given over his life gladly to the service of the Savior. Now he writes such things as you see there, and the other boys all laugh."

"That is not right," said Joseph softly, "but they are only boys, all of them. Boys are full of tricks, Agent."

"Indeed they are!" cried Monteith, puffing up again. "And I will tell you about just one of those tricks."

"Do that, my friend. My ears are uncovered."

"Well, this past Christmas we celebrated the birth of our Lord by making a little stable scene with the manger, and so forth, in Bethlehem. Of course, there was the little pack mule tied as the faithful ass beside the sleeping babe. And do you know what some monstrous boy had done to the innocent brute?"

Joseph shook his head wonderingly. "I could never imagine," he said. "Tell me."

"He had taken . . . he had *stolen* . . . some of the mission's whitewash and dappled the rear of that animal to imitate a Nez Percé Appaloosa horse, and had marked in red paint on the two halves of his rump the name, 'Sun Eagle'. Now what do you think of that for your fine boy? He admitted it, you know. It was his work."

My chief put his chin down to his chest. He seemed to be having some trouble with his swallowing. It was as though he had caught a fishbone crosswise in his throat and were trying to be polite about choking on it. But after a bit he was able to raise his head and continue. "I think it is very unfortunate," he answered the agent. "It is true my father tore up the Bible and that I have followed his way, but I will not tolerate Wallowa boys making laughs about your God. What do you suggest we do?"

"Heyets must be punished severely."

"In what manner?"

"He should be flogged."

"Have you flogged him before, Agent?"

"No. Frankly, I've been afraid to try it. The rascal told me that, if I touched him, he would have his uncle, Yellow Wolf, come in and kill me."

"His uncle, Yellow Wolf, is but a boy himself, Agent."

"You do not need to tell me of Yellow Wolf. I know him very well. He has the eye of a mad dog. I wouldn't trust him ten feet away."

"I see. How else have you thought to punish Heyets?"

"He must be made to say the school prayers, on his knees, in front of the other boys."

"Alone?"

"Yes, alone."

"Has he prayed like this before, Agent?"

"Not once. He says he believes in Hunyewat. He says he did not come here to study Jesus Christ. He tells wild tales

47

of the power of Hunyewat to the Christian boys and has them believing that anything Jesus of Nazareth did in 'ten moons' Hunyewat could do in 'two suns'. He asks them such sacrilegious questions as . . . 'Did you ever see a picture of Hunyewat riding a pack mule?' . . . and he has the entire class so disorganized they spend more time learning the Brave Songs, Scalp Chants, and Salmon Dances from him than they do the Sunday school hymns from me. I will not tolerate it a day longer, Joseph. I simply cannot and will not do it. The matter is your entire responsibility, and you must make the final decision on it right now."

Joseph moved his head in understanding and raised his hand for the agent to calm himself and wait while both of them thought a little while.

Presently he went on. "Very well, Agent," he said. "Do you know what my father, Old Joseph, told me about this same school many years ago when he came to take me away from it?"

"I can very well imagine what the old heathen might have said," agreed Agent Monteith. "But go ahead and tell it in your way. You will anyway. That's the Indian of it."

"It is," replied Joseph, "and here is the way my father told it to me. He said . . . 'My son, always remember what I am about to say. A school is a good thing when it teaches school thoughts from schoolbooks. But the place for God and for His book is in the church. Pray in the church, if you wish, and choose the God which pleases you. But in the school, do not pray. In the school, work hard all the time at the printed thoughts of reading and writing and of the white man's way of figuring with numbers. Do that six days, and on the seventh day go to church and pray all you want.' "

"Your father was a very wise man," admitted Agent Monteith, "until he left the church."

48

"He was a wise man after he left the church, too," said Joseph. "And here is the rest of his wisdom which you did not allow me to finish. The old chief finally said to me . . . 'But, my son, when the time comes that they will not let you learn your lessons except at the price of kneeling to their God, when they demand of you to become of their faith before they will give you a schoolbook, or feed you your food, or allow you your decent shelter from the snow and cold, then that is the time to tell them that they do not follow the way of their own Lord Jesus which He taught in the Holy Land two thousand snows before our little time here upon our mother earth. I once believed in Jesus Christ, the Savior,' said my father, 'and I know his words as well as any agent. It was not His way to ask for payment, neither before nor after He gave of Himself or of His goods.' "

"In heaven's name," fumed Agent Monteith, breaking in again, "what are you trying to say, Joseph?"

Joseph answered him very quietly: "I am trying to say that it is not my way, either."

After that, both men stood a considerable time staring right at each other.

"Well," said Agent Monteith at last and somewhat nervously, "that is scarcely anything new. You have not been in church since your father tore up the Bible on this same spot eleven years ago."

"That is not what I mean, Agent."

"All right, all right, what is it that you do mean?"

"I mean about the boy."

"What about the boy?"

"I am doing with him as my father did with me when they would not teach me unless I prayed first."

"Joseph, I warn you!"

"It is too late for warning. All has been said. It is you

and I who have failed, Agent, not this child. There is nothing he can do here. In his way he is wiser than either of us. He knows he is an Indian and cannot be a white man. I am taking him back to his own people, Agent. You will not see him in this place again. *Taz alago.*"

I could not have been more stunned. Since I knew the importance of my position at the school, I had been waiting to learn what kind of punishment would be agreed upon as the terms of my staying there. Yet, instead, here was my chief taking me proudly by the hand and leading me out of that log-walled schoolhouse there at Lapwai, Idaho, in the severe winter of 1875, without one more spoken word of parting, or rearward glance of consideration, for powerful Indian Agent John Monteith.

I will say that it was a strange and wonderful feeling. Thrilling to it, I got up behind Joseph on his broad-backed old brown traveling horse, and we set out through the falling snow toward the snug teepees along the Imnaha River where, since the most ancient one could remember, our Nez Percé people had spent their winters.

In all the long way home Joseph and I said not a word to one another, and that, too, was the Indian way. As he himself put it, all had been said back at Lapwai. Now was the time for riding in rich silence and, if a grateful Nez Percé boy remained of the old beliefs, for offering up a final humble word to Hunyewat.

So it was I bowed my small head behind Joseph's great shoulders and said my first prayer in five moons.

So it was I ended my Lapwai winter.

Winter Shadows

Foreword

He was a very small and homely boy of mixed Mandan and other blood, a wandering orphan adopted by the band of the old Mandan chief, Black Cat. His name was Kagohami, Little Raven, and in the beginning there was no pride in that name for him. The Mandans had given it to the boy because of his peculiarly dark skin and feathery short black hair—skin and hair certainly not that of a pure Indian inheritance.

Because the boy looked different, he *was* different. He was not a real Mandan and was not treated as a true member of the band. Yet in the end his tribal foster father, Cheyenne Man, taught him to be proud of his mixed blood, taught him, also, that a boy of any blood may win the battle, if only his heart be unafraid, his spirit unflinching. How Little Raven fought his battle, and against what overwhelming odds, is the burden of this tale.

In the land of the Mandans, the elders still touch their foreheads with respect when they speak of its small hero.

"Ai-hai!" they say, their old eyes shining. "There was a *real* Mandan, that boy Kagohami! Come closer to the fire. Sit down. Let us tell you how it went with him in that winter of the Big Cold, when but for his young faith there would have been no Mandan people. . . ."

One

The winter came hard to the land of the Mandans. The blizzard wind stalked and cried among the log-walled lodges as if it were some great white starving wolf from the far Arctic. Not even the old chief, Black Cat, could remember a cold period as fearful and prolonged as this one. He watched his people's supply of firewood dwindle with each freezing hour. He saw the stores of parched corn and dried buffalo beef disappear. Finally he knew that he must call one more meeting of the council of elders. A last decision toward the survival of the village must be made.

Late in the Moon of December, Black Cat sent for the head men to gather at his big lodge. With these wise ones of the tribe to the dwelling of the chief came one who was neither an elder nor a sage. He was, in fact, a very small boy. When Black Cat saw the youth entering the council with the old men, his weathered features grew stern. This was no business for boys. The Mandan people faced hunger and cold. Their gods had deserted them, and only the Blizzard Giant waited for them after the last log had been burned, the last scrap of buffalo meat had been eaten.

"Little Raven," said the old chief, "what are you doing here?"

The small boy made the sign of respect toward his chief

and answered quietly: "My uncle sent me. He said I was to represent him in the council. May I take his seat?"

Black Cat looked at the old men of the council. "What do you say?" he asked them. "Do you wish to sit in council with a child of but eleven winters?"

"Of course not," answered one of the elders. "Such a thing at a serious time like this would be unheard of. Why do you even suggest it?"

"I don't suggest it," denied Black Cat. "I only ask you what you think."

"I think it is foolish," said another of the elders. "Tell the boy to leave the lodge at once."

But a third member of the council objected. "No, wait a moment," he said. "We haven't even asked the boy his opinion yet. Since when do we make a judgment without hearing what is to be heard? At least permit this child to say why it is his uncle has sent him here to take his seat."

Little Raven knew this speaker, but from a distance only. He was an old, old man, so heavy with years that no other Indian could remember his age. He had seen a hundred winters, some said, and some said more than a hundred. Some said, no, it was ten less than that. But none of them truly knew his years. They only knew that, when he spoke, they respected him, and they listened.

"All right," the first elder said. "Go on. Ask the boy why his uncle sent him to the council."

The ancient warrior, whose name was Cheyenne Man, turned his head toward Little Raven. The glow of the firelight fell upon his snow-white hair and the thousand wrinkles of his face. To Little Raven he looked as old as the bluffs of the river, as the rocks of the hills. But his words were clear and strong.

"Do not be afraid, boy," he said. "Tell us in your own

way why your uncle sent you here. Why did he not come to the council himself?"

"Thank you," murmured Little Raven, making the sign of respect toward the incredibly old warrior. "The truth is that my uncle is too weak to walk, and too cold to talk. We have only four sticks of firewood remaining. We have eaten nothing the past three days. I am only a small boy, but I am all my uncle had to send to the council in his place."

Cheyenne Man looked around at the other elders. One by one the older men of the village nodded to him and made the sign of acceptance. The chief, Black Cat, also nodded.

Cheyenne Man reached out his hand, touching the curly dark hair of Little Raven.

"Take your uncle's place in the circle," he said. "When the body freezes and the stomach shrinks, eleven winters can become as seventy."

Two

~

Little Raven believed the council would never end. But he was being honored by the wise ones of the village, and he remained quiet, not fidgeting about or asking questions. Neither did the old men ask any questions of him. They only talked of bygone times.

With their words they journeyed far back into the history of the tribe, seeking reasons for the present troubles. They spoke of the brave days when the Mandans had been the most powerful tribe on the upper river. That had been in the time before the smallpox sickness had fallen upon them, reducing their number to less than two hundred people. They talked longingly of the good years when old Black Cat, the father of the present Chief Black Cat, had begun the trade with the French and the English and of how that trade had made the Mandans rich beyond all the other Indians. Yes, and happy. But the elders were honest in their memories.

The Mandans had never really recovered from the terrible plague of the white man's "spotted fever", the smallpox. The many wanderings of the Mandans, after the great sickness, had further weakened and scattered the tribe. Also the buffalo had become scarce, driven away by the white hide hunters, who came to replace the beaver trappers of the old days. Each spring it became harder and harder to find the big herds of former times. Then had come the time of the Indian agent and the reservation, when all of the Indians were told to live and be content and to stay in one place.

This last, sad thought brought the elders to that most recent moment in tribal memory when their own small band, surely among the last free remnants of the once-great Mandan people, had returned to the ancestral upper river lands. Briefly, sorrowfully, they spoke of their efforts to live the old life, to rebuild the old ways, to make the name of Mandan a proud thing once more. But too many of the people had grown old. Too many of them had lost the spirit to try, and the young people did not seem to care if they were Mandans or mud hens, or whether they lived in freedom or upon the reservations. Only the old men remembered and cared. And it was now the oldest of these old men who held up his gnarled hand and recalled his comrades gently from their journey into the past.

"My chiefs," reminded Cheyenne Man, "let us talk of this winter we face now, not of those other winters which have gone."

His companions looked at him, made uneasy by his chiding.

"That is an easy thing to say," grumbled one of them. "But fine words won't fill our empty bellies. Neither will cold wind."

"True, true," nodded Cheyenne Man. "Yet men must plan and talk together, or they perish. Come, why are we starving?"

Subdued by his calmness, the others tried to answer him.

The snow had come too early and was too deep. The deer and the elk could not be hunted. The Missouri, their beloved "Mother Stream", had frozen completely across in the September Moon. The fat perch and catfish, the succulent mallard and gray goose, all of the river's usual food things, had thus gone ungathered.

The cold had grown so severe that the ponies had needed to be brought into the lodges, sheltered there, and hand fed with willow bark and tender small boughs of alder. As well, shelled corn had to be given to the younger horses. Soon the ice coat in the forest had become so heavy that no knife or hatchet might cut the bark or chop the juicy boughs to feed the soft-eyed, splendid ponies for which the Mandans were noted.

More shelled corn being necessary for the horses, less of that corn was left for the people, who then ate more meat. The meat ran low. Soon it was nearly vanished. Now the ponies became hungry, the Mandans starved, the warm, snug lodges of chinked mud and poles grew cold, and the end was not far.

The old men smoked many pipes, prayed many prayers. They thought of more reasons why the village had reached its dire state. They told more stories to one another of how it was the will of the gods, the work of the Blizzard Giant, and they could do little about it. We must be brave, they told one another. We must go back to our lodges and tell our women and children to be brave. What else might they tell themselves, or their waiting families, they asked one another?

It was here that Cheyenne Man stood up from his place in the circle. He stood very tall, and Little Raven saw that, while he was sad, he was also angry. His fine old face was hard as the ice itself, and he looked about him at his comrades of the council with his dark eyes on fire.

"My brothers," he said, "there is one thing which we can

tell ourselves, even if we do not tell our loved ones. And that is the truth."

"What is that you say?" demanded Black Cat. "Are you calling us all liars? Do you hint that we are less than men? That we sit here and tell falsehoods to ourselves?"

The chief was angry, and Little Raven feared for Cheyenne Man. But Cheyenne Man had seen many battles and sat in many councils. The indignation of chiefs was not new to him.

"Black Cat knows as well as I what it is that has brought us to our terrible plight. All of you know it. Don't blame the gods. Don't blame the Blizzard Giant." Cheyenne Man stared at the elders, accusing each of them and all of them with the look. *"Blame the whisky,"* he said softly. "That's why our women and old ones grow weak. Why we sit here making excuses. Why even eleven-year-old boys must come to sit with us, when their uncles or their fathers or their grandfathers cannot rise to walk from cold and hunger. It is the whisky. Nothing else. It has ruined us."

At this, the elders broke into denials. They spoke loudly, but it did not sway Cheyenne Man. He repeated his charge that, when they should have been out hunting and fishing and planting and harvesting, the men of the band had been buying and drinking the white man's whisky. This was the downfall of their village, he said, and not the hard winter.

To Little Raven this talk of whisky did not seem so odd or so strange as it might to some white boy of his age. He had seen the men of his tribe made into wild things and devils by the poisons of the trade whisky that was the curse of all Indians. The Mandan youth understood what whisky did, even if he did not know what whisky was. Or why the men drank it. Or why they would trade or sell anything that they owned for just a tin cupful of the vile-tasting fluid.

Little Raven was *afraid* of whisky. He had seen it melt the legs of warriors and confuse the brains of wise men. Whisky was a bad thing.

But the old men of the council did not want to admit this. They refused to agree with Cheyenne Man. Each vowed that he himself never touched the white man's evil juice, would not think of buying such wicked stuff. Yet Little Raven knew all of them drank whisky, even Black Cat. Cheyenne Man seemed free of its power. Little Raven had never seen his legs turn to water or his brain to mush. But then Cheyenne Man was a very unusual Indian, different in many ways from the other elders and from Black Cat, the chief.

Still the old men would not say that whisky had betrayed them as Mandans. They would not listen to Cheyenne Man, either, when he called upon them to confess who it was that sold them the whisky. They all denied they knew any such a being. A whisky seller? In their midst? Nonsense. It must be that Cheyenne Man's brain was affected by the cold. They knew of no whisky seller. They could point to no one living in that land of theirs who traded the evil liquor.

"Very well," Cheyenne Man told them. "If you will not say you are wrong, no one can help you. But even now there is the odor of whisky upon some of you in this very lodge. Why do you lie to me? Why do you lie to yourselves?"

Black Cat did not care for such talk. "There will be no more of this." He scowled. "We do not lie to you. Why should we? Besides, what good would it do to admit anything? Would that destroy the whisky seller? Would it break his brown jugs? Spill his whisky? Would it bring back our ponies that have starved? Would it return the flesh to the bones of our people? Would it bring back the gay laughter of our cold and hungry children?"

"No," said Cheyenne Man, "it would do none of these things. But it would do something else. It would bring back the furs the Mandans traded the whisky seller for his brown clay jugs of whisky. And with those furs we could go to the trading post at Turtle Mountain and get food for those furs. Turtle Mountain is a long journey, agreed. It is almost to the Land of the Grandmother. But we could go there and get food if we had back our furs to trade for it."

Black Cat knew this was true. But he also knew that it did not matter now. "No," he answered. "It is too late for that. You speak with a brave but hopeless tongue. Return to your lodges, my brothers. Say to the people that it is too late to do anything. Tell them to pray harder for the help of the gods."

"Bah!" cried Cheyenne Man. "It is never too late to try!"

With the angry words, he clasped the hand of Little Raven and turned away.

"Come, boy," he said softly. "Perhaps there is some small thing which we may yet do for your poor uncle."

The old warrior strode out of the lodge, chin high, never glancing back at his fellows. Little Raven felt very proud. He, too, raised his chin and walked with foot firm to the earth. For some reason it did not seem to him that he was still only a boy of eleven winters. He seemed to have grown as tall as a pine tree just from the touch of his new friend's hand.

Three

When they came to the lodge of Little Raven's uncle, the boy stood aside so that Cheyenne Man might enter first. But when he went to follow his new friend inside, Cheyenne Man made a motion with the fingers to the lips, as though to warn that the uncle was asleep. Little Raven was uneasy. He felt something in the lodge, something which had not been there when he left.

"What is it?" he asked. "Why do you halt me from going near my uncle?"

"Your uncle is deep in sleep, boy. He will awake no more. You must come and live with me."

"No, no!" Little Raven's cry burst from him without thinking. Leave his uncle who had been his only father and his only mother—his entire family—all his brief life? Such a thought could not be. The boy tried to elude Cheyenne Man, to slip around him and run to his uncle's side. But the tall, white-haired elder held onto his shoulder.

"You will obey me, boy," he said, "now and hereafter."

"No!" shouted Little Raven, the tears running down his cheeks. "This is our lodge, my uncle's and mine. If he sleeps in it, then so do I."

"Your uncle was an old man, boy. He needs to sleep. You are very young, a good, bright boy. You must not sleep in this lodge where the Dark One has been."

It was then that Little Raven understood what it was he had felt in the lodge. He looked up at Cheyenne Man, very frightened, his voice small.

"But I have no other family. I am an orphan now. Who would want me?"

"I would," said Cheyenne Man. "From this moment in your uncle's lodge, I am your father and you are my son. Come."

Little Raven's heart grew warm that such a fine and important man would want to be his father. Yet he could not accept his great fortune. His uncle had been a poor man, a bad hunter, and a whisky drinker. Food and the other things of life had never been plentiful in his lodge. The lodge itself was the smallest and the poorest in the village. Little Raven was a very dark-skinned boy with large head and thin body. Quite small for his age, he was marked with a certain cast of features and waving, curly black hair not like the other Mandan children. Accordingly he had always been something of an outcast in the band. He was "different", and the other children did not permit him to forget it. He was not mistreated, of course. The Indians accepted all of the band as equals. It was just that Little Raven did not really know what it was—except that he was very surprised that a man of importance in the tribe's councils would genuinely welcome into his home such a small and ugly boy, and one so poor.

"I don't know," he said at last, stepping away from Cheyenne Man. "I am grateful, but you have your own family to worry about. One more mouth to feed will only weaken your lodge."

Cheyenne Man nodded his head. "Give me your hand, Little Raven," he said. "Come and see my lodge. You have never been inside it. There are many things there you do not know. Things I wish to tell you of. Things you should hear about yourself, and about me, so that you may be brought to understand why it is that you were permitted to sit in council, and why I ask you to come and live with me as my son."

Little Raven looked up at the gaunt elder. He was puzzled by what Cheyenne Man had said. But he was interested by it, too. Still, he had his pride, and he knew the tribal rules.

"How may I come with you when I have nothing to bring with me?" he asked. "No single gift or offering thing to bring with me to your lodge? Even a poor Mandan must bring something."

"Of course, he must," agreed Cheyenne Man. "Do you think I would ask you to come if you had nothing to bring with you? Bring your four sticks of firewood, boy. Don't stand there feeling sorry for yourself. You are rich and do not know it."

So it was that the tall old warrior and the small Indian boy went out of the uncle's lodge and away through the snow. The old warrior carried a stone pipe in a leather case, the symbol of his eldership. The young boy carried four sticks of firewood, all the household belongings he had in the world. Yet in the proud way that they walked, it was understood they were two very wealthy men.

Four

The lodge of Cheyenne Man was a wonderful place. After the fashion of the Mandan round house, it was constructed of a circle of peeled logs driven upright into the earth. Upon this circle a roof of poles, willow branches, prairie grasses, and chinking clay was fastened. This made a sort of low-topped beehive dwelling that withstood the fierce heat of summer and the deep cold of winter alike. In the center of the great inner room, the fireplace was built of glazed clay and river stones. Above this hearth, a hole in the roof permitted the escape of the wood ash and smoke, while the warmth of the burning fire stayed within the lodge. Every part of the wall, each inch of the floor, was covered with the skins of animals. When such a snug fortress was decked with fresh balsam twigs to sweeten its fire-lit air, as was this fine home of Cheyenne Man's, then it was a veritable chief of lodges.

Yet the greater surprise was yet to come to the staring Little Raven. When his new father had brought him through the narrow entrance way of roofed logs, the Mandan boy shook his small head in disbelief.

"It is beautiful, my father," he said. "But it seems so lonely. Have you no family at all, Father?"

"That is part of the story I wanted to tell you." Cheyenne Man nodded. "It is part of the reason I wanted you to come here with me and see my home." He paused, taking Little Raven's hand in his own. "Come, let us go to the fire, boy. Let us place upon its small remaining heat your four sticks of wood. We shall make some willow-bark tea, and I will cook you a shred of pony meat that I have saved."

At the mention of this meat, Little Raven's face grew sad. "I see that your horses are all gone, my father. That is a sorrowful thing. I know that you loved them. We had no horses, my uncle and I. But what a far worse thing to have them and then be forced to use them for food."

"The horses have kept the people alive, boy. The gods will reward our ponies."

"And what will our people do for horses in the spring, my father?"

"Little Raven, if someone does not find us other food, or bring us help in some magic way, our people will not need horses in the spring."

"Oh, yes. That, too, is a sorrowful thing, my father."

"Yes," said Cheyenne Man. "But come, now, no more sad talk. To the fire at once, boy! I want to tell you a story . . . it's the one I promised you . . . about you and about me. Is that all right?"

Little Raven looked up at him. The firelight flickered on the craggy old face, the silver-white hair, the dark skin and fierce eyes of the ancient warrior. The boy thought he had never seen such a grand figure, and such fine pride.

He tightened his small hand upon Cheyenne Man's large one. "Yes, thank you, my father," he said, standing straight. "Let us go to the fire and forget sad things. We are both Mandans. We are not afraid."

The old man nodded again. It was probably a trick of the firelight, but it seemed that a tear glittered for a moment upon his wrinkled dark cheek.

"We are both *more* than Mandans," he said softly. "Come, let me tell you how that is true."

Five

"Many snows ago but still within my lifetime," the ancient warrior began, "there came to the land of the Mandans a wondrous band of strange white men. These white men were from far south down the big river that we call Mother Missouri. They were from farther south than any Mandan, or any Indian of any tribe that we knew, had ever been.

"There were four times ten of these travelers. Most of them, except for their French boatmen, were soldiers. They had two chiefs with them. One of these chiefs was named Lewis. The other one was named Clark. That one of the chiefs who was named Lewis was thin of body and had soft brown hair, and him we called Quiet Chief. The other chief, the one named Clark, was strong and wide of body. He had bright eyes and fiery hair the color of the sun when it pauses upon the rim of the prairie just before it goes to rest in the big blue water to the west. This one we called Red Head Chief, and he was the one we all respected. What a chief he was!

"He could outshine, outrun, out-hunt any Indian. He was a man among men. Yet he was extremely gentle. He always had a smile and a happy light in his eyes. He never bothered our women, and he was forever kind to our children. Now this Red Head Chief owned a great black man for a slave. The black man's name was York, and he was nearly seven feet tall. He had the muscles of the grizzly bear and the short curly hair upon his great head like that of the bull buffalo. Remember the name of this black York, Little Raven, for you will meet with that name again very soon.

"Ah, what a remarkable creature, that black York! He was amazing. We Mandans had never seen such a man before that time. And we have surely never seen one since."

Cheyenne Man paused a moment to tamp his pipe. He put another ember to its bowl, puffing to get the tobacco lit once more.

"Now," he continued, "these white men, with their two captains, told us they came from a village called Wah-shing-tahn. They said they were the soldiers of the big chief of that village, who was their father and the father, too, of all the Indians, except those who lived to the north in the Land of the Grandmother. They said we Mandans must make peace with our enemies, the Sioux. They said that all the Indians, the Mandans, Sioux, Minnetarees, Arikaras, Pawnees, Omahas, and Missouris, all of them, must obey their great new father and fight no more, the one with the other."

Cheyenne Man got up from the fire and brought his war bag from the rear of the lodge. He took from it a gleaming medal hung upon a faded ribbon of scarlet red. When the light of the fire struck the medal, Little Raven saw engraved upon its face the hand of a white man and the hand of a red man meeting in the grip of peace. Also there were two crossed tomahawks and some words in the white man's tongue. Anyone could see that it was a very great medal.

"This was given to me by Red Head Chief," announced Cheyenne Man with quiet pride. "It was from Je-fer-sahn, our great new father. I was a young man then, and a tribal chief. I lived in the village of Matootonhas, the first village

71

upon the river where the white men arrived from the south. If you will look in the writings of the two captains, you will see my name there with all the others. It stands second only to the great Shahaka, who was to journey westward with the white captains in their search for the vast blue water where the sun sleeps at night."

Pausing once more, Cheyenne Man smiled. "Excuse me, boy," he said. "An old man is easily taken aside from the main trail. I have gotten a little away from your part in this story. Now be patient and you will see."

"Of course, my father," said Little Raven. "But I was not impatient. A good story always takes time."

"Wisely put," said the old man. "Now, let's see." He puffed harder upon the pipe, eyes closing again, as he tried to peer backward into the past. "The Mandans promised to keep the peace. So the white men journeyed on. But first they must have a guide, as no man, red or white, had ever been up Mother Missouri so far as they were going. As if from the gods, a young Indian girl came from out of the morning mists on the river. She was in a canoe with a Frenchman named Charbonneau, who traded with us Mandans. Her name was Sacajawea. She was a captured Shoshone. It was her fierce people who stood between the white men and the blue water of the West. Sacajawea, who many have called Bird Woman but whose name meant Canoe Woman in the tongue of her people, was only of sixteen summers in age. Just a child. But she went with the white captains, and but for her they would never have returned from their perilous travels over the Big Rock Mountains.

"Now, Sacajawea and black York and Charbonneau, the two captains, and their soldiers, all of them are dead and gone. They sleep and dream of the great times when they came among the Mandans bringing peace and freedom from their father in Wah-shing-tahn to all the Indians of Mother Missouri.

"But the part of this which you must know, Little Raven, still lives. It is young, as you are young, and it will never sleep. I tell you, because I was there and knew all of these people and knew of their lives, that in your body flows the blood of both York and Sacajawea, and also of the Mandan chief, Shahaka, who was Chief Red Head's greatest Indian friend. York's blood comes from your father's side, Sacajawea's from your mother's side. You are *more* than a Mandan, Little Raven, and you need bow your head in the presence of no Indian. If you are but a poor boy, and an orphan who also does not look quite right to his Mandan relatives, never despair. These are things of pride, not shame. To bear mixed blood is a blessing, not a curse, for straight blood runs narrow in the veins. When a man is of many fathers and many mothers, he is all the more a man. Do you understand that story, Little Raven? Will you remember its lesson?"

The old man finished his tale and sat waiting for Little Raven's reply.

The boy was puzzled. "You speak of a man, Father," he frowned. "I am only a boy."

"Yes, my son, but a boy becomes a man. Then he will be no more and no less than he was as a boy. The twig makes the tree. A tall pine and unbent grows not from a mean seed and twisted."

Still frowning, Little Raven shook his dark head. "But I am also still an orphan. I have no true father and mother. I do not know, even, who my father was, or my mother. You, at least, had a family. You had a father and a fine mother, and it was easy for you to be a brave boy so that you could

73

grow into a brave man. You make me proud when I listen to your tale of the proud blood that is in my body, but I am still a poor orphan boy in my mind. This being so, and all of the Mandans knowing it is true, how can I ever be as you, my new father?"

Cheyenne Man looked at him, peering through the thinning wreathes of the tobacco smoke from his pipe. "Ah," he said very softly, "did I forget to tell you? I am sorry. You see, I, too, was an orphan boy."

"What is that you say, my father?"

"Yes, I was the same as you. The Mandans took my mother as a slave. She died while I was still too young to remember her. I never knew my father, either. They called me Cheyenne Man after my mother, who was of that tribe."

Little Raven felt his heart pound with pride. The great Cheyenne Man had been an orphan boy like himself? A poor boy who never knew his own father? Or remembered his own mother? Ah, what a fine story this was, after all.

"Thank you, Father," he said to the elder. "Now I understand your words. Now I feel like your true son. Now I have a home, at last. Now I am not an orphan any more."

The old warrior nodded and said to him in a very low voice, trembling a little. "Neither am I an orphan any more. Thank *you*."

Six

After the story of black York and the Shoshone slave girl, Sacajawea, of noble Shahaka and the two American captains of Je-fer-sahn, had been told, Little Raven was filled with great pride and contentment. For as long as it required Cheyenne Man to prepare the willow-bark tea and warm the final scraps of stringy pony meat—all of the food and drink remaining to the old warrior—Little Raven was happy.

But then, when the tea was drunk and the pony meat scraps chewed and swallowed, the fire commenced to die down, and the big lodge grew cold. Putting the last of his four small sticks of firewood upon the graying embers, Little Raven huddled deeper into the wolf's fur jacket Cheyenne Man had put about his shoulders. His mind returned soon enough to the fate awaiting the Mandan village.

"Father," he said, "have all the ponies been eaten?"

Cheyenne Man shook his head. "No," he said. "There are seven of them in the lodge of Knife Eye."

"Knife Eye, Father? The Assiniboin medicine man?"

"Yes, do you know another Knife Eye, boy?"

"I do not want to know another one, my father. One is bad enough. I am afraid of him, I think. *Ih!* Such an unpleasant fellow. I don't think I would want him caring for my pony."

"*Shhh,*" commanded Cheyenne Man. "Knife Eye has great power. He seems able to hear what is said in all the lodges. Besides, his medicine is greater than any Mandan's. He has kept the ponies fat, just as he promised. Meanwhile, all the other ponies have starved to ribs and hollow flanks and gone into the boiling pots."

"How does he do this, Father?"

"No one knows. Knife Eye says it is because the Mandans are weak from the peace they have been keeping for the dead American captains of Je-fer-sahn. He says that his people are strong because they have stayed at war with the Americans. Since he shows his magic powers to our people by keeping their ponies alive, the Mandans are afraid of him. You fear him yourself, boy. You have only now said so."

"Yes, that is a true thing."

"But why, Little Raven? Shall I tell you? It is because he *does* have strong medicine and we do *not.* No man may fight the gods and win."

"Are you afraid of Knife Eye, Father?"

"Yes."

"Oh, I didn't think you feared any man."

"Medicine men are not like other men. They work for the gods. Why else do you think we Mandans did as Knife Eye said with the ponies?"

"What did he say, Father?"

"That we should select the finest six mares and the one best stallion of all the pony herd remaining to us, and then entrust them to his care. He alone could bring them through the winter alive. Could feed them until the new grass came again and the big ice was gone once more from the river. He has done it, too. All of the ponies are alive and even putting on flesh in this terrible cold. It is great magic. More than that. For myself, I owe him a debt I cannot pay. The stallion chosen from them all was my own beloved gray racer, Bright Arrow."

"I see." Little Raven paused, frowning. "But why does it have to be magic, my father? Maybe Knife Eye has some real horse feed hidden away in some secret place."

Cheyenne Man's face grew stern. "Boy," he said, "you must not talk like this against Knife Eye."

"But I'm not talking against him, Father. I am saying that feeding ponies does not have to be magic."

"Be quiet, boy. You know nothing of such things."

"True, Father. But it was not I of whom I was thinking. It was my poor uncle who has gone to sleep. He always said there was no such thing as magic, except inside a whisky bottle. Do you think Knife Eye is feeding the ponies with a bottle, Father?"

"No more, now, do you hear me, boy!" Cheyenne Man was uneasy. His tone was sharp. "Horses can't live on whisky. Besides, Knife Eye is the one Indian I know, other than myself, who does not suffer from the white man's fiery curse. He tastes no drop of the vile poison. I have never smelled it upon him, or seen him with a brown clay jug or a tin cup in his hand. He is strong, as I am strong."

"Yet you fear him, Father. Why?"

"Because of his magic."

Little Raven would have pressed the questioning, but at this point Cheyenne Man let the lad understand that he would listen no more. It had grown colder in the lodge, and it was time to seek the sleeping furs. They must burrow into the buffalo robes and wait for another sun to warm the freezing world.

When the boy had obediently snuggled into his sleeping robes by the side of the dying fire, he looked across the popping embers to where Cheyenne Man was pulling his own furs and blankets around him.

"Father," said Little Raven quietly, "may I ask one last thing about our people?"

"Of course, boy," said the old man. "I did not mean to be harsh with you. What is it?"

"Well, Father, it is this . . . if the people find no more food, will they eat the seven ponies of Knife Eye?"

"Yes, no magic is as strong as the pinching of a man's belly."

"And when the seven ponies are eaten, Father?"

"Then the people will lie down in their sleeping robes and yield to the Blizzard Giant."

"Is there no single hope, Father? No way at all in which to save the people? *You* must know a way."

Cheyenne Man lay quietly for a long moment, thinking of the boy's innocent faith in his age and strength and wisdom. He was deeply affected. Moreover, he did think he knew of something that might be done, even though there was no real hope of doing it.

"Yes, my son," he answered finally. "I do know of one way in which some chance might be given the people. But we are all too weak, or too old, or too severely frozen now. None of us could undertake the journey. We discussed it in the councils before today. We even tried it two times. But each time it was exactly as Knife Eye predicted it would be. The men who we sent simply disappeared. We followed their tracks northward only a short way before they vanished, and the men were not seen again. They were good men, too. One of them, Hard Shield, was an older warrior, strong as an oak tree growing in rock. The other was a younger man, Two Elk, also strong and a fine hunter and tracker. If such men could not reach the Red Coats in their full strength before the hunger and cold had weakened their limbs, then no man could reach them now."

"The Red Coats, my father? Who are they?"

Little Raven's curiosity was aroused. His imagination caught at the name "Red Coats" and would not leave it. There was something about that name and about the fact that once it had meant hope to his starving people. He knew he had heard that name before. It made a memory sound in his thoughts. Yet he could not recall it now.

"Please, Father," he repeated, "who are the Red Coats?"

Cheyenne Man answered with increasing drowsiness.

"They are men of magic, also, my son. They are the soldier police who ride horses in the Land of the Grandmother and who never tell a lie. They are white men but very fair, always, to the Indians. They are called Northwest Mounted Police by their own people. No man of any skin color who has done a bad thing ever escapes them."

"Oh, yes, now I remember about them." Little Raven smiled. "They wear the bright scarlet-red coats and shoot the rifles which never miss. They make everyone obey the law up there in the Land of the Grandmother."

The Land of the Grandmother was the Mandan word for Canada, taken from the fact that the English queen, Victoria, was called "the grandmother" by the Canadian Sioux cousins of the Mandans. In truth, this country lay overly far from the river lands where Little Raven lived, in the Dakotas, on American soil. But the imagination of an eleven-year-old Indian boy reduced the many miles to nothing. Little Raven was much aroused by the thought of the scarlet-coated Canadian horsemen so respected by the red men and so feared by all bad men, red or white. He spoke again of this interest to Cheyenne Man, but the latter did not respond. In his excitement, Little Raven did not notice this. He had been taken by a sudden and great inspiration.

"Father," he said, eyes shining, "suppose some Mandan might yet find his way to one of the Red Coats up there in the Land of the Grandmother? What trail would that Mandan need to take to reach their camp? How would he set out to go to the camp of the Red Coat police from our village?"

"Eh?" grunted the old warrior, half arousing and opening one sleepy eye. "What is that? How to find the Red Coat police from our village? Well, if you could find some Mandan with that much heart remaining, that Mandan would need to start along the trail toward the Turtle Mountain trading post. And when the trading post was reached, that Mandan would have to inquire of the traders as to the trail on across the boundary line into the Land of the Grandmother. That would be the trail leading to the place where the Red Coat police are camped up there. I understand that it is not too far from Turtle Mountain, but, of course, I have never been there myself. Now to strike that old trail which goes from our village to Turtle Mountain that Mandan would need to start out north along the river for a little way, but then, suddenly, there is a place where the trail . . . where it turns away . . . and goes . . . and goes to the . . . ."

"Father!" cried Little Raven. "Please! Don't stop now. It goes where, Father? You follow the river north a little way until what? Father? Do you hear me?"

But the boy's calls went unanswered except by loud snores. Cheyenne Man was fast asleep.

Seven

Once the thought had entered Little Raven's mind, the Indian boy moved quickly. He moved silently, too, for he dared not awake Cheyenne Man. From the lodge of his new father, he borrowed certain things he must have to make his far journey. He took the wolf-skin jacket he had worn by the fire and also an old chopping axe with a partly broken handle, which Cheyenne Man used to trim firewood inside the lodge. The axe, he placed in his knife belt, along with the small hunting blade his uncle had given him on the day of his seventh year. The bulky jacket of wolf fur, with its hood and high collar, he pulled on over his own warm winter clothing. He was ready then.

On tiptoe, he went out the entrance way of the lodge. Outside, he found his snowshoes, where he had left them upon entering his new home. Putting them on, he set off through the swirling snowflakes toward the bank of the Missouri River.

Coming to the river, he set off up its bank, going northward. The last of the village that he saw was the lodge of the medicine man, Knife Eye. It was the last lodge on the outskirts of the village, set apart from all the others, looking black and sinister through the thickening fall of the snow. Little Raven shivered a bit as he looked at that lodge. He

was afraid of the medicine man, as were all Indians. To
have magic power was all right, thought Little Raven, except that one never could depend upon what the medicine
man would do with that power. If he made good medicine,
fine. But if he made bad medicine . . . *ih!* One must be very
careful, then.

Thinking thus, the Indian boy made a large circle in
going past the lodge of Knife Eye. No use leaving his tracks
where the medicine man could see them. Even if the snow
was filling up those tracks most quickly, it was not safe.
When a man had magic power, he could see right through
snow, or anything else.

Now, with the lodge behind him and only the friendly
path of the old trail leading away along the river toward
where it must turn off to Turtle Mountain and the Land of
the Grandmother, Little Raven felt far better. He had no
doubt he would find his way to the trading post and the
friendly traders of Turtle Mountain. There, he knew, the
white men kept a big store of goods which the Indians of
both the American and Canadian tribes depended upon re-
ceiving in exchange for their furs and buffalo robes and
sometimes a few of their ponies, or some moccasins, bas-
kets, tanned deer hides, elk-horn spoons, and other things
which the Indian women were skilled in making.

When he arrived at Turtle Mountain, he would inquire
at once about the trail leading onward to the camp of the
Red Coat police, which his new father had told him was not
far, at all, into the Land of the Grandmother. And he would
go on up there to that camp and tell the Red Coats about
the poor starving Mandan people of his village. Then one of
the Red Coats would leap upon his great horse. He would
seize up Little Raven and carry him before him on the
saddle of the great horse. Or perhaps it would be behind

him. Little Raven did not care which it was. He knew that, either way, the brave Red Coat would bring help to the starving village, and he would bring Little Raven back to the village along with that help. The people and his new father, Cheyenne Man, and the seven last ponies in Knife Eye's lodge, yes, and even Knife Eye himself, would all be saved. And he, Little Raven, would be a hero in the land of the Mandans for a hundred winters. Maybe even more.

Well, Little Raven was only a very small boy. It did not occur to him to worry about the manner in which the Red Coat would save the Mandan village. The way in which the Canadian policeman would carry back to the village all the food and firewood that its people needed to keep them from starving and freezing was not Little Raven's concern. The policeman would think of some way. The Red Coats never failed.

Besides this faith, the Mandan youth knew one other thing that kept him going. It was a thing that he had heard Cheyenne Man say in the council of elders. It was the thing of which his new father had so angrily reminded Black Cat—*the fact that it was never too late to try.*

Little Raven nodded to himself at this proud memory. He struggled even harder against the rising power of the wind. He was determined that he would repay his new father for his good heart and for his kindness to a poor boy of mixed blood, who was only a part Mandan.

Strengthened by this vow, the tiny Indian youth fought his way into the ever-deepening snows. As he did, the blizzard wind howled louder and with a fiercer sound. It carried a terrible cold in its sharp teeth of ice and snow. It snapped at the heels of Little Raven. It bit at the tip of his nose and the lobes of his ears. Breath came hard. The air was so cold it burned the lungs and glued together the nostrils. Little

Raven panted and struggled on. The river trail was growing still deeper with the piling snows of the returning blizzard. But the boy did not despair. He only remembered Cheyenne Man and made another vow—if the gods would only grant him some small luck, Little Raven would continue with his cold journey.

He would never stop. He would fight the snow and the ice until there were no more strength and no more heartbeats remaining in him. All he asked was just a small amount of luck.

But the gods did not grant Little Raven such luck. As he rounded a turn in the riverbank path, a dark figure loomed suddenly before him. It was an Indian man, with a rifle, dressed in heavy furs and wearing snowshoes. He came from the other direction, from the direction of Turtle Mountain, and he stood in the track, now, barring the way of Little Raven.

The Mandan boy stopped. For some reason he was afraid of this Indian man. He felt as though he had seen him before. Yet one could not be certain under all those winter furs and with the deep hood of otter and fox fur that covered the man's head and hid his face.

But then, even as his heart pounded and he did not know whether to stand or to flee, the dark figure laughed in a friendly way and threw back the hood of his coat. It was the medicine man, Knife Eye.

Eight

~

Knife Eye did not say anything at first. He only stood in the trail and smiled at Little Raven.

But the boy grew fearful. Knife Eye was not a Mandan. He was an Assiniboin Indian. His people were savage and war-like, noted for their cruelty as for their treachery. They were not admirable warriors like the Sioux or Cheyennes. They were not brave like bears, but skulking, vicious, and silently deadly like wolves. As a medicine man, Knife Eye traded strongly on this reputation of his people. It added to the fear in which the Mandans and the other northern Indians held him. He was thus able to use his power with greater effect. Also, even if he was a fierce-eyed man, he professed to be the friend of everyone. At the moment, too, he was smiling upon Little Raven with all the warmth of a fine winter's sunrise. Perhaps, thought the weary boy, he was wrong about the medicine man. It might be that Knife Eye would not harm him. Perhaps he would even help him.

"Good day, Knife Eye," he greeted the medicine man carefully. "May I share the trail with you? I would like to get past. I am going to the north."

Knife Eye's face seemed to freeze for a moment. But then his fine sunny smile melted it quickly. "Ah, boy, to the north, you say? And why would you be setting forth in that

85

direction in such a bad storm?"

"It is to save my people," answered Little Raven. "I am going to Turtle Mountain to bring the Red Coats."

"What is that?"

"My new father, Cheyenne Man, told me that if I could bring back a Red Coat, the Red Coat would save our people from starving and freezing."

"He said that to *you?*" Knife Eye's smile was gone from his scowling face. "He told such a tiny bug of a mixed-blood boy to go and fetch the Red Coats?"

"Well, no, he did not say *I* could do it. He said, if someone could do it, the village might be saved."

"Ah, yes," said Knife Eye, the breath whistling out through his front teeth. "Come a little closer to me, boy. I cannot hear you so well with all this wind."

Little Raven started to obey. Then he saw a look upon the wide face of Knife Eye that he did not like at all. "No, thank you," he said politely. "I must be going, anyway. It is a long way to Turtle Mountain. Excuse me."

He started to go around Knife Eye, but the medicine man seized him by one arm. Knife Eye was a huge Indian, strong, thick of body, and very tall. His grip was like a band of steel.

"Wait a moment, small friend." He laughed. "Don't you know what happened to those other Mandans who tried to go to Turtle Mountain? Didn't your new father tell you about them?"

"Yes, he did. Please let go of my arm."

"And you think your medicine is stronger than that of Hard Shield and the other man . . . Two Elk . . . who disappeared on this trail to Turtle Mountain?"

"No, but I am only a boy. What god would harm me?"

"A god, you say? That is very funny. All you Mandans

leave everything to the gods, don't you?"

Little Raven drew himself up tall. "I am not a Mandan," he said. "Only a little part. I am of the blood of black York and Sacajawea. That is strong blood. It is American blood, Cheyenne Man says. And that is the very best blood, he says. *Ih!* I fear no gods."

"Good for you," said Knife Eye, his scowl easing away. "Now, if I let you go, will you go at once home to the lodge of Cheyenne Man? Will you behave and do as I say?"

The big Indian's hand pained the arm of Little Raven. But the boy was stubborn, and he would not lie.

"No," he said. "I have given my word to go to Turtle Mountain. Let me go or Cheyenne Man will have something to say to you. I will show him the marks you are making on my arm."

"Aye," answered Knife Eye, "that new father of yours is of a tribe which fights. The Cheyennes are not like the Mandans, who only talk and pray. I will have to be careful with that old fool."

"Do you call my new father an old fool?" demanded Little Raven.

"Of course." Knife Eye laughed again and twisted the arm of Little Raven.

The boy did not cry out, however. Instead, he put his free hand inside of his bulky wolf-skin winter coat and loosened the rusted camp axe he had borrowed from the lodge of Cheyenne Man. Knife Eye did not notice the small hand slide inside the big coat.

"Now, boy," he growled in his deep voice, "you have brought real trouble to yourself. You won't obey me. You threaten to tell your new father that I bruised your arm. You will not turn around and forget about going on to Turtle Mountain. Too bad, too bad. . . ." Knife Eye frowned, as if trying to think just what he must do. Suddenly he asked the young captive: "Did your new father know you set out for Turtle Mountain and the Red Coats?"

"No," replied Little Raven. "He was asleep."

At once he could tell he had made a terrible mistake. He saw the cruel grin that twisted the face of Knife Eye. He saw the rough hand reach for the huge hunting knife in the scabbard at Knife Eye's belt. He felt the other strong hand tighten on his aching arm like the talons of a hawk.

"Ah." Knife Eye smiled. "What a sad thing for you."

"What are you going to do?" cried the boy, alarmed.

"Only what I must do." The other shrugged. "You see a gun makes too much noise. Someone might hear it and come to see what happened. The knife is like a serpent in the grass. It slides in and disappears without a sound."

"Knife Eye! You would not slide such a weapon into me?"

The powerful Assiniboin did not answer the boy's frightened cry, except to pull out the shining blade of the knife. But that is all he did with the knife. For the blade had no sooner cleared its scabbard than the hand of Little Raven also came out from beneath the loose fur of his big coat. In the boy's hand was the old broken axe from Cheyenne Man's lodge.

Knife Eye had only time to see the axe, but not to avoid it. He gave a curse but was too slow. Before he could move his big, broad feet, Little Raven brought down the blunt end of the hatchet squarely on the toe of the medicine man.

Knife Eye bellowed with the great pain of the blow. He made a cry that sounded like that of a grizzly bear squalling with its foot in a saw-toothed trap. At the same time, he seized the wounded toe in both of his hands and began dancing wildly about.

To accomplish this, he had to drop both the knife and Little Raven's arm. Instantly the tiny youth dodged past the big Indian and was gone away up the Turtle Mountain trail, running like a snowshoe hare. Before Knife Eye might even think to cease yelling and dancing in pain, the Blizzard Giant had covered up the tracks of the fleeing Mandan boy, and he was safe for that moment.

Nine

Little Raven had no idea how far he had come along the trail. He only knew that the wind was driving more savagely than ever, that the cold was becoming deeper and deeper, the snow piling higher and higher. In truth, he could not even see the trail any more and did not know where it was—or where he was. He stopped still when this realization came to him.

It was a frightening thing, being lost in a great blizzard. It was as a bad dream. There was no way to run because one could not see more than a few feet in any direction. There was no hope in calling out for help, as the howl of the storm was far greater than any boy's human cry. It was growing dark now, making things even more terrifying.

Little Raven lost his courage. He began to run, even if he did not know the way. To run and to cry out. It was all he could do, he thought. It was better than standing in the middle of the Blizzard Giant's freezing-cold belly doing nothing.

The boy could not see anything, so thick was the swirl of the snow about him. Again and again he fell, again and again regained his feet, and plunged onward.

But at last he fell into deep snow, and he did not get up again. Instead, he kept on falling downward and downward into a greater darkness than that of the storm. Then, suddenly, he was no longer falling through white snow but had landed with a hard thump on hard earth. The landing shook his breath and left him gasping. Yet in a moment, being an Indian lad and hardy of bone and limb, he recovered himself and tried to peer about him in the darkness. He could see absolutely nothing.

Beneath him, he could feel with his hand that he was seated on sand. It was dry sand and warm. It came to him that he had fallen into some kind of a cave beneath the riverbank and was safe and sound. He could have a good sleep in that fine cave, then find his way out when the new sun came. But quickly he realized that he could smell, even if he could not see, and what he was smelling was a wild animal scent, its odor strong and rank in his nostrils! Then he could hear, as well as smell, and what he heard was the slow panting of some large beast. The animal's breath, the licking of its chops between pants, the sound of its moist saliva between tongue and teeth, all came to him with chilling distinctness.

In another moment, his peering eyes becoming adjusted to the thick blackness of the cave, he could see at last. What he saw were two slanted green eyes gleaming like hot fire. They stared steadily at him from a distance no greater than the outreaching of a man's arm. As they did, Little Raven heard a low and rumbling growl that made all the small hairs along the back of his neck stand straight on end. It was then that he recognized the animal smell so strong in his nostrils, then that his heart almost stopped beating with fear. It was the smell of the killer of the north woods.

He had fallen through the snow's crust into the winter denning place of the great gray timber wolf.

Ten

Little Raven ought to have remembered to say a prayer to the gods, but he did not. He was too terrified. The jaws of the timber wolf were awesome things. They were powerful enough to break the bone in a grown man's leg, or to snap through the heel tendons of a bull moose, or elk, or even a great buffalo in one instant, crippling the huge animal and bringing it to the earth. But a strange thing happened with this wolf. It did not attack Little Raven. Instead of springing at him, it stopped its deep snarling and began sniffing the darkness.

Little Raven held as still as a fawn in a thicket. The wolf's sniffing drew nearer to him. Suddenly the moist nose bumped his face. He could feel the hot panting of the wolf's breath against his cheek. Then the nose shifted to his hands, his feet, finally settling into his wolf-skin coat.

In a flash the answer to the animal's confusion came to Little Raven. It was the fact that he was such a small boy that the borrowed wolf-skin coat covered nearly all of him. The wolf must think that he was some odd new kind of a brother—a wolfling that did not smell just exactly right, but that still did smell wolfish and was covered with wolf fur.

By this time Little Raven's eyes had grown accustomed to the darkness of the den, and he could see a bit. What he saw first was the wolf itself. The big beast was sitting directly in front of him. It was squatting on its haunches, its red tongue lolling in and out just like a friendly dog. It cocked its huge head from side to side, studying the Indian boy with obvious curiosity.

What was this strange-looking thing in the wolf fur that smelled like a wolf but did not have a tail or sharp ears? It reached forth its nose once more and took another inquiring sniff of Little Raven's wolf-skin coat. To the Mandan boy the animal seemed to be trying to decide if he were good to eat or not.

He did not know what he ought to do. But Indian boys were taught from babyhood all of the animal and bird sounds of the prairie and of the forest, and, when the wolf whined deeply in its throat, Little Raven knew that it was a friendly whine. He did his best to imitate the whine in answer to the wolf.

The wolf then made a new, low, grunting sound in its chest. Again Little Raven imitated the grunt as best he was able. It seemed to be good enough.

The wolf got up from its haunches and licked the Indian boy's face. It uttered another low growl.

Little Raven could not imitate this growl, so he did not try to answer it. However, some other things in that warm dark cave did answer it. Little Raven heard their whimperings and tiny squealings. He knew by instinct what was making the sounds and why his life had been spared.

This was a mother wolf with little ones. Because she was nursing whelps and because the wolf always had the most powerful of mother instincts for taking an orphan young thing to its breast, this mother wolf had accepted Little Raven. More than that the low growl that had just alerted her cubs was an invitation for Little Raven to come and join the family—to snuggle in among the wolf's own whelps and be as one of them.

Little Raven had heard Mandan legends of wolves adopting lost human babies. It was true that he was rather a well-grown "baby" of eleven winters. In any case, the Indian boy did not question his great fortune. He crawled obediently across the sandy floor of the cave to where the wolf cubs lay huddled in their nest of leaves and dry grasses. Wriggling in among them, he made himself into as small a ball as he might, hoping that his wolf-skin coat covered all of him and that the mother wolf continued to think he was one of her kind.

Evidently she did. She came over to her nest and smelled each of the true whelps, smelled Little Raven, then simply gave a satisfied grunt and lay down so that her young ones could nurse her breasts.

In this position her head lay against Little Raven's thigh. He put out his hand and patted her warm fur. She growled, and licked his hand. He could hear her tail thump the sand as she wagged it gently. By that he knew all was well, that the mother wolf would never harm him now. He lifted her head so that it would lie in his small lap. She snuggled up, grunting again, then relaxed.

"Mother Wolf," said Little Raven, "I am your new child and very weary. Watch over me, please, while I rest and sleep with my brothers and sisters who are your children."

With that, the Mandan boy lay back and closed his eyes. He knew no fear of the wolf or of awakening in safety. The wolf was his guardian and would watch over him and permit him shelter until the storm was past. Only an Indian youth could have believed such a thing, of course. Yes, since he did believe it, he held no fear within him.

Because he had no fear within him, the mother wolf

could scent no fear upon his outer self. She only growled once again when the boy spoke to her with human words. She thumped her tail upon the sand to let him know that she understood what he had said to her, and that she would honor the trust. She sighed and buried her head still more deeply in the Mandan boy's lap and was asleep before he was.

Eleven

In the darkness of the wolf den there was no way for Little Raven to tell the passage of time. The night was as the day, and the day was as the night. But the Indian boy was hungry, and, when his stomach began to draw in from emptiness, he lay down with his new brothers and sisters, the wolf whelps, and took his supper as they did.

The mother wolf was pleased at this. She turned her head and bumped Little Raven with her nose and licked him with her tongue just as she did with her own children. It did not appear too remarkable to Little Raven that a savage she-wolf would adopt him. He took this for strong medicine sent to him by the gods. At the same time, he did not yield all the credit to this strong medicine. He understood that he was very lucky. He knew that without the she-wolf's warm fur and sweet milk he would surely have died in the great storm. So he prayed some to the gods and a good deal more to the mother wolf.

Then, after what seemed to him like many days, the wind ceased blowing and the Blizzard Giant stalked away back north from whence he had come. The mother wolf grew restless and sought to leave the den.

Little Raven heard her whining near the entrance. He crawled to her side and saw that the snow of the storm had blocked the tunnel to the outside. The she-wolf had dug the entrance way partly clear, as the snow beneath the ground's surface was soft. But now she had struck the outer crust, where the blizzard had frozen the flakes into a covering as hard as ice. Her poor blunted claws could dig no more. She panted heavily and whined again to the Indian boy at her side.

Little Raven knew real joy then, for he could help his friend. With the rusted axe of Cheyenne Man, he commenced to hack and chop at the frozen snow. In a short time he had broken through the crust and the tunnel way was opened to the clean air and sunshine of the outer forest world.

The Mandan boy thought he had never seen a day so lovely as that one. He and the mother wolf lay for several moments in the entrance way of the den, looking up at the blue sky and warming their cold paws and fingers by the light of the yellow sun. It was a fine, brief instant, but only that.

The mother wolf was in sad state. She was so wearied by the digging, so worn and weak from the long time in the den without food for herself, that she could scarcely rise to her feet. When she tried to walk, she sank back into the snow and could not rise again without resting. Little Raven knew this for a serious matter, a matter, even, where the Dark One might enter before long if something were not done.

The mother wolf wanted to go out and hunt for food, that she might eat and so make more milk for the feeding of her tiny cubs. She understood by her instincts that if she did not go out and hunt, she would starve, and the little ones starve with her. Yet, all that she had strength to do was whine plaintively to the Indian boy who crouched beside her, his small hand on her head.

Little Raven believed that he understood the whine that she uttered. He spoke reassuringly to the exhausted she-wolf. "Mother Wolf," he said, putting his arms about her neck to hug her tightly, "you have fed me, and now I shall feed you. Return to your babies. Keep them warm. Tell them that all is well. Little Raven has gone for food and will return. Tell the babies my medicine is strong. Let them sleep in peace. Have no fears yourself, dear mother."

The wolf uttered another soft whine, and reached up to lick his face. Little Raven knew that she understood what he had told her, for she at once turned about and crawled back into the den. He could hear the tiny whimperings of the cubs, as they greeted their dam. He listened until he could hear, also, the happy sounds of their small lips wetly nursing and smacking with pleasure at her warm breasts.

He smiled then and made ready. Fortunately he still had with him his caribou-hide snowshoes, these having fallen with him into the wolf den. It was but the work of a moment to don the shoes. Then he settled his lucky axe in his inner belt, tightened the wolf-skin coat, and set out through the deep, wind-blasted snow toward his home with Cheyenne Man in the village of the Mandans.

For such a small lad, and one not strong, the task of finding his way home after a great blizzard might have seemed impossible. But it was no such thing in reality. Little Raven was entirely calm about the prospect. Once the snow had stopped falling and the wind ceased to blow, there was no unusual trick to it. All one had to do was to establish which way the streams ran. Then he would know which ways were north and south. Also, he would need only to follow whatever stream he first encountered to the south, that is, go along its bank southward. The stream would join

Mother Missouri before long—all of the streams did that—and then it was a simple matter of following the big river on south to the village of Black Cat's band.

Little Raven smiled once more to himself. He kicked at the snow to make sure his shoes were laced on properly and tightly. Then away he went, skimming as lightly as an owl feather over the hard crust.

All going well, the poor mother wolf would have her lean empty belly full before another darkness came. Had not Little Raven said it? *Ih!* Of course, he had. Hold firm beneath the foot, blizzard snow. Spring to the stride. Make swift the light steps of Kagohami, the Little Raven of the Mandans. Was his heart not pure, his purpose in the right? These things being so, could he fail? *Ih!* Never!

Twelve

Little Raven had not gone as far away from his village as he had thought. It seemed to him almost no time before he came again to the Mandan lodges. Soon he was standing proudly in front of the surprised Cheyenne Man. The white-haired warrior greeted him with great happiness. He had feared him lost in the great storm. Now he held him close and patted his dark hair, doing that so he might not weep, or make any other sign of weakness, which the boy would think less than manly.

When the greetings had quieted, Little Raven dutifully told his new father the story of his adventure. He asked that Cheyenne Man pardon him for leaving without permission, explained that he, Little Raven, had thought only of trying to find help for the starving people and not of disobeying his new father. He reported the full story of the mother wolf and of his vow to return to her with food. About his frightening experience with Knife Eye he said nothing. He did not think that Cheyenne Man would approve of striking the Assiniboin medicine man with the firewood hatchet. He would only worry about it, and Little Raven wished to spare him that. Little Raven also wished to spare himself any possible willow switching for daring to assault such a powerful and feared man. So he kept silent about Knife Eye.

Concluding his task, he repeated to Cheyenne Man the urgent need for returning with food to the mother wolf.

"I owe the wolf my life, Father," he said. "No Indian could deny such a debt. Will you help me to discharge it?"

The ancient warrior shook his head sadly in reply. "There is only one trouble, my son," he said. "How will we bring food to the mother wolf when we do not have any food for ourselves? The small shreds of pony meat which we shared before you departed were all that we had."

Little Raven's face darkened in sorrow. "Is there nothing at all we may do to find food, Father?" he asked anxiously.

"Perhaps I can think of some way." Cheyenne Man fell silent with hard thought. But after many minutes he could think of nothing to help the mother wolf, and Little Raven could wait no longer.

"Father," he said, "I will take my dead uncle's bow and arrows. I will go back out into the snow, and I will hunt until I find a winter hare, or grouse, or even a bunting. I would rather freeze than dishonor a friend."

Cheyenne Man nodded again, but he was frowning. "You must learn that big words do not fill empty bellies," he said sternly. "No hunter goes forth in weather such as this. My old bones warn me that another blizzard is coming very soon. You would not be so lucky this second time. No, my son, the mother wolf and her little ones must starve. I cannot let you go forth again. I forbid it absolutely."

"But, Father, I gave my word!"

"You gave it foolishly."

"Never, my father. I will go and ask the chief for food. Black Cat will give me some small scrap." Again Cheyenne Man shook his head. "My son," he said, "it is for ourselves that we must go and beg food of Black Cat, not for any wolf and her cubs."

"Let me speak to the chief, Father. Let me tell him how the wolf suckled me at its breast. How can any Indian refuse such an obligation to a forest brother or sister?"

"Very well," agreed Cheyenne Man, not able to deny the hope shining in Little Raven's dark eyes. "Come with me. Tell your story to Black Cat. Perhaps he will see the debt as your young eyes see it."

When they had gone to the chief and told him the story, Black Cat only shook his head precisely as Cheyenne Man had done before him.

"Boy," he said, almost angrily, "how can we think to give good food to the forest creatures when we are starving for a decent bite ourselves? As a matter of fact," he added, turning to Cheyenne Man, "I believe that we must ask your new son to show us where this wolf den is. You will understand the need which is in my mind."

Cheyenne Man nodded but looked quite unhappy. Not knowing what the older men were speaking of, Little Raven patted his new father's hand.

"Do not be unhappy," he smiled. "I can easily show you the way to the mother wolf's den. There is no trouble in that."

"You do not understand the trouble that is in it," answered Cheyenne Man. "Black Cat means that we must capture your mother wolf and her babies and put them into the boiling pot."

Little Raven could not believe his new father. He looked hard at Black Cat.

"How could a chief do such a thing?" he demanded hotly. "You would betray that poor trusting mother and her furry babies? You, the chief of the Mandans? No, it cannot be. You must tell me that my father did not understand you."

102

"He understood, boy. Now you be still a moment."
Black Cat's voice was deep with feeling, and Little Raven
fell silent. In a breath or two, the chief continued soberly.
"It is you who do not understand, Little Raven," he said.
"The wolf is our brother, that is true. The buffalo also is
our brother. So is the black bear, the grizzly bear, the deer,
the antelope, the elk. So, too, even, are such as the crow
and the snake and the turtle. But when man is dying for
want of food to eat, he will eat his own brother, be it buffalo
or toad, tender deer or friendly wolf. Now the Mandan
people are near to dying. Do not speak to your father and
your chief in haughty tones of honor and obligation. Go
and prepare yourself to lead us to the den of the mother
wolf. Say no more, not one word, against your elders here."

Little Raven started to ignore the chief's warning. He
opened his mouth to issue some angry words of his own.
But Cheyenne Man promptly closed that small mouth by
placing his large hand over it.

"My new son understands," he said quietly to Black Cat.

Then he took Little Raven by the arm and led him forth
from the chief's lodge in such manner that the boy's feet
did not touch the earth, but trod the air aimlessly.

Outside the lodge, the old warrior put the boy down and
said to him gruffly, giving him a final rough tug: "Come
along, boy. You and I must have a little talk."

Thirteen

Gently, but with great firmness, Cheyenne Man told Little Raven how it must be. "You know, boy," he said, "that I also love the creatures of the forest. But this time it is different."

"To the mother wolf it is no different," maintained the small youth stubbornly. "Her life means as much to her as my own life means to me."

"That is not the idea, boy."

"What is the idea, then, my father?"

"It is that the gods placed the forest creatures on the earth for the Indian to eat. Do you think he placed the Mandan children here for the animals to eat them?"

"Well, Father, sometimes they do eat us."

"True, but you twist my words. You make me appear wrong."

"You are wrong, Father. So is Black Cat. But I am right."

Cheyenne Man smiled a little then. "My son," he said, "you have a head harder than a river stone. However, I admire your spirit of loyalty."

"I only know when I am right, Father, and others wrong."

"This, too, may be true. But your rightness will not save

the mother wolf and her babies. Soon Black Cat will come for you. You will have to go with him and the hunters to show them where the den is."

Little Raven understood he could not alter this fact. He was but a boy and could not withstand his chief and his gentle new father. But he knew that if a strong old pine tree sometimes broke under a fierce wind, the slim young willow bent skillfully and stayed unbroken. In this way, then, he spoke in a low voice to Cheyenne Man.

"I am very weary, Father," he pleaded. "Can you not go to our chief and request of him a little time? You see, I ought to have a sleep before going forth again. Remember, I am but a weak thing of eleven winters only. A boy must have his rest, Father. Else how may I lead the hunters when they come?"

"A true thing." Cheyenne Man nodded gravely. "I shall go at once and tell Black Cat to wait until you have had a nap."

He started out the entrance way of the lodge, then paused. "Boy," he said sternly, "no more running away now."

"Only so far as the lodge of my uncle," said Little Raven. "I want to get the bow and arrows, which are now mine. Even a boy of eleven winters ought to have a bow for hunting."

"All right. But I want you back here in this lodge when I return."

"I will do my best, Father."

Cheyenne Man studied him a moment, smiling a little. "Well, I don't know now, boy. Your best can be pretty unusual. Perhaps you had better just give me your honor word that you will be here when I return."

Little Raven at once drew himself to his full height. He

stood almost to Cheyenne Man's belt. "Father," he said, "when did I ever lie to you?"

Again the old warrior smiled. "You have scarcely had time yet," he said. "But I understand your pride. I withdraw the pledge. Be quick in going to your uncle's lodge. That new storm I smelled is coming even sooner than I thought. *Ih!* How cold it grows!"

The old warrior bent his tall form and went out of the low entrance way. When he had safely gone, Little Raven took up the chopping hatchet once more, and donned his big wolf-skin coat. In the way that he belted the garment so carefully, and in the tight way that he laced on his snow-shoes outside the log tunnel of the entrance, it was evident he intended to travel much farther than his uncle's lodge. The same intention was made plain by the manner in which he moved through the village streets.

He kept his fur hood pulled far forward over his face. Taking a roundabout course, he did not go directly to the abandoned home of his boyhood. Rather, he went from lodge to lodge on the way there. Behind each lodge he would stop and wait to see if any Mandan had spied him out and might be following after him. He must be crafty as the lynx and the coyote, now. All depended on his sudden plan, and, if the plan of Little Raven was somewhat bad, it was also brave and bold.

It was not a good thing, the boy knew, that he must tell a falsehood to his new father. But he believed in his heart that what he now meant to do was an honorable thing and would excuse the falsehood. At least he knew that what he meant to do required a good deal of courage. It could scarcely be otherwise when an eleven-year-old boy planned to enter the medicine lodge of Knife Eye to steal food for the mother wolf!

Yes, that was the plan. Little Raven knew, when the chief of his Mandan band told him there was no food in the village, that there was food just outside the village. Knife Eye was not starving. He looked big and strong. He must have food hidden in his lodge. Besides, was he not a man of magic? Could he not create his own food with his powerful medicine? It seemed so to Little Raven. The moment he had thought of the daring plan to rob Knife Eye, he had told himself that it was not like stealing from a fellow Mandan. Moreover, the boy was still a bit angered at the medicine man's rough treatment of him, and he was too young to appreciate the very real danger he might be in, should Knife Eye catch him in the medicine lodge.

He was, to be truthful, behaving very foolishly, and very recklessly. Yet his heart was strong, for he believed that honor demanded he repay the mother wolf for saving his life. If to do this he must lie and steal, then he was ready to do these bad things. Surely the gods would make his people understand that he was right in doing them. Surely, when all was over, the tribe would honor him. For Little Raven did not intend to take food just for the mother wolf alone. He intended to take more food for himself, so that, when he had fed the wolf brood, he might continue on his journey northward to Turtle Mountain and the Red Coats.

He had been most unwise to set out without food the first time and in the middle of a big storm. But this time it was going to be different. This time he would have food, and, in spite of his new father's warning, he did not think any second great storm was coming. Besides, this time he would take great care not to meet up with Knife Eye. No one else would know where he had gone, either. So no one else would come after him, or try to stop him. It was all very simple, really.

Such were the thoughts which kept running through the boy's mind as he reached the lodge of his uncle, took up the bow and arrows, slung them across his back, set out once more toward the lodge of Knife Eye near Mother Missouri, the big river.

When he reached the lodge, the sureness of his actions faltered. The lodge looked black and eerie. It was very still. No smoke curled from its chimney hole. No sound came from within its log walls. The wolf dogs of Knife Eye's sled team were not in their usual places, staked on chains in the snow. They were gone along with the sled. By this, Little Raven knew that the medicine man was out in the forest and not at home. His heart grew steady once more. Taking one final look all about the riverbank to be certain that no Mandan from the village was near, he went across the open snow. At the rear of the lodge, he waited again, listening with his ear against the cold logs. He heard no sound inside the lodge. Quickly, then, he slid around the circular wall and came to the entrance way. Saying a quick Mandan prayer for good luck, he raised the entrance skins and slipped beneath them, into the dark entrance tunnel beyond.

Crawling on hands and knees so that his head would not accidentally strike the low roof and make a noise, he came to the inner room of the lodge. A quick look showed him that his luck prayer had been answered. The only ones at home in the lodge of Knife Eye that day were the seven beautiful ponies of the Mandan village. These, smelling Little Raven's Mandan scent, were only too pleased to see the small boy. They whickered in a friendly way from their willow pole stalls in the rear of the big lodge and pricked up their sharp ears to let him know they recognized him.

Little Raven let out a great sigh of relief. "Hush, hush,

dear ponies," he said softly. "I am glad to see you with your coats shining and your ribs not showing. But do not whicker any more. Knife Eye might hear you."

The beautiful horses appeared to understand what he said, for they fell still and merely watched him with great interest as he moved about the lodge.

After only a little moving about, the Mandan boy grew sorely puzzled. As large as the medicine man's lodge was, it was strangely empty. There was none of the things in it that Little Raven had supposed he would find there in such huge supply. There was not even a little wood for the fire. There was no meat or corn, no green sticks or willow bark for the ponies to eat.

Little Raven grew very nervous. Much time was passing. Soon Knife Eye might return, and Knife Eye did not like little Mandan boys. Especially ones who came to rob him in his sacred medicine lodge!

Fourteen

The lodge of Knife Eye stood upon a rocky point that jutted high above the bank of the river. In front of the lodge was only the river. Behind it, and upon each side, lay the open prairie and what Little Raven called "the forest". This was the scanty bordering of timber that ran along the banks of the streams of that great upland plains country. The Assiniboin River trail ran past the lodge, trending northward. The trail to Turtle Mountain also ran along the river but soon veered to the northeast, away from the great stream. Across the Missouri from the lodge began the rolling sweeps of the buffalo pastures. Beyond the grassland, westward, were the Black Hills, and beyond the Black Hills, far, far beyond them, waited the fabled Big Rock Mountains, where dwelled the mysterious Snake Indians and where no Mandan Indian had dared to go.

To the Indians of all the local tribes, the rocky point of Knife Eye's lodge was taboo. This meant that it was sacred ground and that no Indian might set foot upon it without permission from the medicine man himself. Knife Eye did not readily grant such permission. Indeed, he almost never did.

Occasionally he would have some of the important chiefs or influential elders come to his lodge and sit in front of it

and smoke. Black Cat and a few of the head men of the
other bands had also been inside the lodge a time or two,
seeking the services of the medicine man and paying outra-
geous prices in valuable furs when they did so. But no man
visited that lodge when Knife Eye was not there, and no
man visited it when he was there, except when he had been
invited.

Now Little Raven, the mixed-blood boy in whose veins
ran the heritage of Sacajawea, Shahaka, and the great
Negro, York, now *he* stood within this forbidden place upon
that forbidden rocky point of the river's bank. Small
wonder, then, that the boy's knees trembled and his
stomach felt small and shaky. Small wonder that he jumped
at every least sound while he searched the lodge for hidden
food, and the time grew longer and longer and longer.

Finally, having found no scrap of food for the mother
wolf or himself, he turned to leave the lodge. As he did, the
slender Mandan ponies pricked up their ears again. In a
moment, they all began to whinny excitedly. In a moment,
Little Raven, holding still as a rabbit, heard the yelping and
growling of Knife Eye's sled dogs. Then he heard the medicine man's deep voice cursing the dogs and ordering them
to be quiet while he chained them.

The boy knew he had no more than a few minutes—the
time it would take Knife Eye to stake out the savage dogs—
in which to make his escape from the lodge. Yet how might
he do this? The only way out was the entrance tunnel, and
Knife Eye staked his dogs all about the exit of that route.
Neither could he dig out under the walls of the lodge, nor
hide behind the ponies, or wish himself invisible. He was
trapped.

All that he might do was to wait for Knife Eye to enter,
then plead with him to spare his life. This was useless, too.

No one knew that he had come to the medicine man's lodge. He had circled and made a clever track line from the village so that he could not be easily followed. He had planned very well. He had been very daring. He had lied to his new father. Now he was going to pay for all of this.

Still, it was not in his nature to give up or to beg. It was in him to keep trying until the last, just as Cheyenne Man had told Black Cat that a man always ought to do.

Thinking thus, his roving eye fell upon a possible hiding place. It was there where the entrance tunnel joined the lodge. Some of the roofing logs had been cut long so that they protruded into the room, making a sort of storage shelf above the curtain of skins which closed off the inner end of the tunnel. Upon this crude shelf the medicine man had placed some old hides, dog harnesses, bits of chain, animal traps, pony bridles, ropes, and such things. Little Raven believed that if he could scramble to this refuge and make himself small enough, he might not be seen. At least it was a better chance than pleading.

Taking off his snowshoes, he threw them up onto the shelf. Then he climbed up the log wall, and snuggled alongside the snowshoes as deeply as he could into the dark recesses of the shelf. There he lay as fearfully as the spruce grouse in its overhead retreat when the hunting panther prowls beneath. He was not a heartbeat too soon.

Growling and grumbling to himself, Knife Eye strode into the big room of his lodge. He halted so close to the hidden Mandan boy that the latter could hear his loud breathing and smell the rank odor of his perspiration. Little Raven was so helpless with fear he could not swallow. He merely rolled his eyes upward and prayed hard to all the gods he could think of, and then to a few he invented just for the moment's urgent need.

For the space of two or three breaths it did not seem that the prayers would work. Outside the lodge, the sled dogs would not quiet down, especially the fierce leader, a great, yellow-eyed brute named Chaka. Knife Eye yelled at the dogs, then went outside and yelled at them some more. "What is the matter with you?" he shouted at them. "What is it you are trying to tell me? You, there, Chaka, what are you yammering about? What is it you scent?"

That is a strange thing, thought Little Raven. *With all that magic he has, he cannot even understand what his own sled dogs say to him? What a remarkable thing.*

But if Knife Eye did not understand his sled dogs, they understood him. With the whip he beat them cruelly until they were silent, then he came back into the lodge.

"I would swear," he said to the Mandan ponies, greeting him with their soft whickerings, "that someone has been here. The dogs smell something, and so do I."

The evil-looking medicine man stood in the center of the room sniffing the air. His glittering eyes swept into every corner, every shadow, each stall of each pony—anywhere that an enemy might hide. But he saw nothing, and no one. The shelf above the entrance way he did not even glance at, for a man could not squeeze himself into that narrow space.

After a long moment, he said to the ponies: "Well, perhaps old Chaka smelled a wolf. Be patient, little ones. I know it is time you had your supper. What beauties you are. What prices you will bring when the snow is gone, and all the Mandan fools with it!"

As Little Raven watched, the medicine man went past the pony stalls toward the rear of the lodge where he had his bed. This bed was laid upon a platform of peeled split logs, very handsomely trimmed, raised somewhat up off the earthen floor. It was covered with the finest sleeping robes of buffalo calf and Arctic white wolf. Little Raven thought he had never seen such a bed as this one, and, indeed, he had not. Neither he, nor any other Indian lad.

Reaching the sleeping platform, Knife Eye quickly swept the furs and robes from it. The next moment he leaned down and raised up the platform, revealing it to be, in fact, a trap door leading to what mysterious vaults Little Raven could not begin to imagine.

The Mandan boy's eyes shone brightly. He held his breath. Was he about to behold the fearful secret of Knife Eye's legendary magic powers? Was this the place he kept his great medicine?

Fifteen

Knife Eye was gone down into the secret place beneath his sleeping robes for only a brief time. When he popped up again through the trap door, he bore an armload of firewood. He disappeared into the hole again, after dropping the wood on the floor of the lodge. In another moment he reappeared. This time he carried a large woven-grass basket brimming full of dried corn. This, too, he sat upon the floor by the hole, diving once more out of sight. The third time he came up out of the hole, he carried a choice piece of sun-cured buffalo beef—a strip of back fat and tenderloin. Little Raven's mouth watered so freely at seeing this feat that he nearly choked on his own saliva. Only his intense interest in watching Knife Eye prevented him from coughing or making some other noise that would have given him away.

The medicine man now closed the trap door and returned the sleeping furs to their places atop it. Going to the pony stalls, he gave each of the Mandan horses a generous scooping of the dried corn from the grass basket. The munching and grinding noises of the hungry ponies devouring the yellow kernels were welcome sounds to the hidden Little Raven. They made it so that it was not so eerily still within the lodge of Knife Eye so that Little Raven might move his limbs a bit and breathe more naturally.

115

Knife Eye put the wood on the fire, boiled his tea, and ate his buffalo beef.

While he did this, it began to grow quiet within the lodge once more. It was dusty up on the shelf by the entrance tunnel. The dust was getting into the nose of Little Raven. It tickled his nose and made the tears come to his eyes. He was about to sneeze.

Burying his head in the hood of his wolf-skin coat, he held his nose with his fingers, forcing the sneeze to discharge "inside his head", as he thought of it. The action hurt his ears and brought pain to the top of his head, yet undoubtedly it saved his life. For when next moment he warily peered out from under the hood, Knife Eye was still eating by the fire. Apparently he had not heard the sound of the muffled sneeze, bless the gods. In fact, the medicine man was in a very good humor.

"Now, let us see, little beauties," he said to the munching ponies, finishing his own meal and standing up. "You have been fed. The fire has been rekindled. My own belly is filled, and the dogs are still fresh and strong." He commenced to get back into his fox fur parka. He picked up his new breech-loading rifle. Into its chamber he put a gleaming brass cartridge from his ammunition belt. He cocked back the hammer. On the shelf over the entrance tunnel, Little Raven shivered.

It was not the cold that made him shake, either. The rifle was simply so wicked-looking and the sound of its loading so deadly. The Mandan boy knew that Knife Eye was going out to hunt some poor creature. He knew, as well, that the medicine man had great power to aim that rifle. He never missed his target. Little Raven's uncle had once told him that Knife Eye needed no other magic than his wonderful rifle, that and his remarkable keenness of vision, which had led to his name of Knife Eye. Now the cruel-faced Assiniboin was going forth to kill an innocent creature of the forest, and that was the thought which made Little Raven shiver. It was even possible, he suddenly feared, that the mother wolf would be the object of Knife Eye's search. Perhaps the medicine man had been to the Mandan village, or had met Black Cat and the Mandan hunters on their way to find the mother wolf and her little ones. Yes, that was surely it. Knife Eye had heard the story told by Little Raven and was going to try to kill the mother wolf himself. But then another thought came to the boy on the shelf. Why would Knife Eye do that? He did not need the food. Moreover, if he had heard the story from any of the villagers, it would not be the wolf he would be looking for. It would be. . . .

Little Raven broke off the thought as it took form in his mind. No, that was a foolish fear. Knife Eye surely had far more important things to do than worry about little Mandan boys.

Below him, now, the medicine man had banked the fire and taken a final look at the seven Mandan ponies. He was ready to go into the tunnel with his gun.

"All right, beauties," he said to the horses in his growling bear's voice. "Be good while I am gone. I do not like to leave you so much alone, but I cannot help it. That little Mandan cub of mixed blood still eludes me. They say in the village that he has been home and gone again." Knife Eye interrupted himself to laugh happily.

It was a happiness that brought the goose-flesh bumps rising up all over Little Raven. Even as he listened to the medicine man going out through the tunnel to harness the sled dogs, his fear increased rather than diminished.

He had been right in his first thought. It was not the mother wolf that Knife Eye sought with his deadly black rifle. It was the Mandan boy, Little Raven.

Sixteen

When Knife Eye had gone, Little Raven lay upon the shelf above the entrance way for a moment. He was trying to think what he should do, but it came to him quickly that nothing had changed. His plan must still come true. Even more so than before now, for he knew where the medicine man stored his food. Even though Knife Eye was hunting for him with the rifle, Little Raven could not forget his vow to the mother wolf.

In another moment he had clamored down from the shelf, run across the lodge to the bed and the trap door. Raising the door, he lowered himself into the hole beneath it, as he had seen Knife Eye do.

The dim light below permitted him to see that he was standing upon the top of a series of steps cut into the soft stone of the riverbank. The steps led downward into what appeared to be a passageway. Down went Little Raven into the lower passage. Following this, he came into a cavern larger than the big lodge that stood above it.

The Indian boy halted in wonder. It was one of the riverbank caves that honeycombed the Missouri in the area of chalky stone bluffs, such as the rocky point of Knife Eye's medicine lodge. Some old, high flood water had eaten away at the bank and left the great underground chamber when the water fell away.

It was evident at a glance that Knife Eye had discovered the cave first. Then he had built this lodge immediately above it, so that he could use the cavern in the secret way of his kind, to help him cheat and steal from the Mandans.

Little Raven could hardly believe what he saw. Down there in the cavern, cool and safe and dry until the next springtime melted the snows, were all of the furs which the people of Little Raven's village had traded for the whisky which Cheyenne Man had told the elders caused the downfall of the tribe. There could be no mistake. An Indian boy could recognize the furs of his band. Little Raven had helped to stretch and cure some of these same skins. He knew, also, what a wealth of furs there were before his eyes. It would easily be enough, even as Cheyenne Man had said, to buy food at Turtle Mountain in quantities to save the entire village.

But how had Knife Eye gotten the furs? He did not sell the whisky. Had not Cheyenne Man told him that the medicine man never was seen to have whisky, never had been known to take a drink of it? Or to have its odor smelled upon his person? Who, then, was the whisky seller? Indeed, where was all the whisky that such a seller would need for trading purposes?

Little Raven was familiar with the glazed brown jugs of hard clay that the white men used to contain the whisky. He had seen more than one of these brown clay jugs in his uncle's lodge and in many others of the lodges of the Mandan band of Black Cat. Even in the chief's own lodge. The small boy understood very well that he had made a powerful discovery of the tribe's furs. Yet he believed he must go very carefully in the way that he brought this news to Cheyenne Man and the people. Knife Eye had great magic. He could make the people afraid to come near the lodge to prove what Little Raven might say of the great cache of furs he had found hidden there. The tribe might even turn upon Little Raven if the medicine man demanded it. No, one must move with extreme care now. One must think very clearly.

He must forget about the furs and the whisky until a later time. He must take some food to the mother wolf. He must take, also, some food for himself. Then he must get out of that secret cavern beneath the medicine lodge of the Assiniboin, Knife Eye, before its cruel owner returned, and he must get to the mother wolf skillfully yet swiftly. He must leave no tracks for either the villagers or the medicine man to follow. He must even fool the savage sled dogs of Knife Eye, especially the fierce Chaka that was said to be able to trail a honeybee through a hard blizzard. *Ih!* He must just stay with his plan, and very quickly, too.

From Knife Eye's plentiful supplies of dried meat and corn, Little Raven took what he needed to fill the big pockets of his wolf-skin coat. Then he crowded some more food, all that he could, into the hood of his fur parka. He was so heavy with food that it was hard work climbing back up the steps toward the trap door. Indeed, he had to pause about halfway up the steps to regain his breath.

It was then that he heard it. One of the ponies whinnied softly in the lodge above him. Then a second pony and a third whickered, as well. They were greeting someone.

Someone had come into the lodge of Knife Eye, someone who walked very heavily, someone who was very large and powerful. Little Raven could hear the slow footsteps move across the earthen floor above him. They were moving toward the trap door. The Indian boy shrank back against the wall of the cavern, watching the opening of the

120

trap door above him. He saw the huge arm reach for the door. He saw the door being lowered. He blinked as it was closed completely and the cavern was plunged into darkness. There was not another sound from above. Little Raven was trapped.

Seventeen

Little Raven had to feel his way back down the steps and into the river cavern. The darkness was not total, but it was so great he could not run. He had to creep like an animal in a burrow. He did not know what he intended doing. He only knew that the trap door was closed, and he could not escape that way. If he were to get away from whoever had closed the door, it must be by another path than the steps to that door.

The boy wasted no time wondering who had been above in the lodge of Knife Eye. The friendly whickering of the ponies had told him that. Since no other Indian dared come to the forbidden lodge, it must be Knife Eye himself. The medicine man had returned too soon. Far too soon. He had come back only minutes after leaving. Why? That was a frightening question, because the answer could mean that Knife Eye suspected that someone had been in his lodge before. It could mean he had known all the time that someone was hiding in his home when he had eaten his food and fed the ponies. But, no. Had he thought of that, he would have searched more thoroughly and found Little Raven. What *was* the answer then? Little Raven did not know.

He did know, however, that should the medicine man find him in the cavern—find out who it was upon whom he had just closed the trap door—then the Mandans would never learn the fate of their small brother, Little Raven.

Now Little Raven was stumbling along in the dark trying to find the other entrance to the river cave. He understood that such an entrance had to exist, or the waters could not have gotten into the earth to wash out the cavern to begin with. But, being so close to the river, would not some light filter through from the other entrance? Would not that other entrance have to be in the bank of the Missouri to have admitted the washing waters? *Ay! Ay!* What a fearful place for a mixed-blood Mandan boy of not yet twelve winters to be!

Little Raven fell over a loose rock. He struck the hard sand of the cave's floor. His breath was driven out of him and a little sense driven in. Wait a bit now.

His uncle had taken him into some river caves exploring for bats and turtle eggs. When they had crawled too far under the ground and could no longer see the light from the opening of the cave, the uncle had known a way to determine the proper direction to retreat. It was very simple. One had only to strike the lighting flint to some dry moss and, when the fire flared up, observe which way the smoke drifted. That way would lie the exit.

Fortunately Little Raven had his fire-making pouch with flint and steel and dried moss at his belt. Along with the rusted hatchet of Cheyenne Man and the old bow and arrows of the uncle, the fire-making pouch had been remembered and taken upon the trail. Weapons and fire making went hand-in-hand. No Indian could survive without both.

Quickly the Mandan boy struck the flint and steel. The sparks flew into the wad of dry moss. When they flared up, he blew upon them, and the small flame burned clearly. In a moment the boy saw the smoke drift swiftly along one wall of the cavern to vanish in a dark cleft opening to the left. As the rabbit leaps to elude the weasel, so he jumped to reach the cleft while the light of his clump of moss lingered against the darkness. He was lucky. He not only reached the cleft in the wall but was able to start upon his way down its narrow passage before the moss flickered out. Then, when its feeble glow had gone, a new light seemed to spring faintly to take its place.

Little Raven stopped and blinked to be sure he was not mistaken about that new light. He was not. It was pale light, and he knew from its color that it was daylight and not firelight. He hurried on down the side passage. In a moment, he had entered a second, smaller cavern. In there the light was much stronger, although quite dim and shadowy still. He could see that, across this second cave, was another short passage with very clear light at its end. *Ah, hi!* Now he knew where he was. Beyond that clear-lighted hole on the far side of the new cavern he could see the frozen breast of Mother Missouri and the dark line of willow thickets that marked its distant bank. All he need do now was scurry across the new cavern, down the last passageway, and out into the blessed open air of the riverbank. What a wonderful ending, after all!

Thinking thus, Little Raven ran out into the new cavern. But there he came to a sudden stop. His black eyes popped wide. *Ih!* Was there no finish to the discoveries of Knife Eye's buried treasure? Look at this!

Little Raven did look at it, and the excitement pounded in his heart. What he saw was that the entire cave sides were built up with log shelves. The shelves ran from the sand floor to the rocky ceiling. They seemed to fill the small second cavern. Each of the shelves, in its turn, was filled with something else, something which had nothing to do with magic but which was certainly very powerful medicine.

The shelves were filled with rows and rows of glazed clay jugs. They were brown jugs with short round handles. They were of a size to hold sixteen tin trade cups of the white man's yellow fire. They were whisky jugs, and Knife Eye, the Assiniboin medicine man, *was* the evil whisky seller!

Now Little Raven understood it was more important than ever that he escape from the river caverns beneath the taboo lodge on Rocky Point. His plan to go and feed the mother wolf and her babies must now be brought off all the more swiftly. He must move with greater speed and skill than even his plan asked of him. For now he knew the secret of the whisky seller. He knew where the furs were with which his starving people could buy food at Turtle Mountain. Now the entire village depended on him.

Very proudly, the boy straightened and started onward toward the last passage. Then a thought struck him. He had to make sure there was whisky in those jugs. If they were empty, Little Raven would make a fool of himself. His punishment, even if not caught by Knife Eye, would be severe. The council of elders would not look kindly on his making lies against the name of Knife Eye.

He went to the nearest of the shelves. To take down one of the jugs required that he put down the bow of his uncle. This he did, leaning the weapon against the cave's wall and seizing a heavy jug. When he shook the jug, it gurgled and made a noise as if filled. But Little Raven could not get the cork out of the neck so that he might smell the contents. He was, in fact, still struggling to do so when the light which had been in the cavern disappeared.

Whirling about, Little Raven could see nothing. All about him was sudden darkness. Then his sharp ears brought him a sound that was more eerie than the blackness. It was the slow, heavy sound of footsteps. The same footsteps he had heard crossing the floor of Knife Eye's lodge, just before the trap door closed.

But these footsteps were not coming from the lodge. These footsteps were coming from the passageway to the riverbank. That was why the light had been blotted out. Someone—or something—very large and heavy of body was in that passageway. Whoever it was—or whatever it was—now panted and breathed like some great silent animal only a few feet away from Little Raven. The Indian youth could distinctly hear the whistle of the thing's breath. He held himself utterly still.

The thing came into the cavern—almost. Little Raven could just make out its blurred form passing in the throat of the passageway to the riverbank. He could sense that the creature was searching the cavern, trying to see through its darkness.

The Indian boy knew that he must in some way get past the creature, and run out the passage to the river. But how was he to do that? If he waited for the creature to hear him, or perhaps see him, then it would be too late. As it was, the boy did not even know if the form that blocked the passageway was an enemy. It might be a friend. But it did not *feel* like a friend.

Little Raven knew that he must attract the creature's attention to something else in the cavern. Then, when it looked in that direction, or moved in that direction, the boy could run for the passage.

The heavy brown clay jug he had been attempting to open was still beneath Little Raven's hand. The boy cautiously raised the jug, careful not to let it touch the floor or the cave's wall. Then, with all his strength, he sent it rolling on its side, as a small barrel, across the cavern's hard and rocky sand. The jug gurgled and rumbled on its way. It struck the far wall of the cave and shattered into a hundred pieces, spilling its contents.

Instantly the form leaped from the passageway toward the sound of the broken jug. As swiftly, Little Raven ran for the patch of daylight he could now see in the passageway where the form had been.

But the creature heard his feet on the sand, and it jumped back into the opening of the passage. Little Raven nearly ran into whatever it was. At the last moment, he was able to turn aside, however, and to dive in under the shelf of jugs just by the passage opening. There he crouched in a tiny bundle of fear, not knowing if he were hidden or if the creature could see him.

The creature, in its time, was making preparations for being sure that it did see him. Little Raven heard the familiar *strinnkkk* sound of flint and steel being struck together. In a moment, the creature had made a light, and it was a big light. Glancing fearfully out from his hiding place, Little Raven realized that the creature had lit a candle of tallow. The shadows jumped and flickered among the rocks of the cave in a way only candlelight had. In the same moment, the creature began to move once again. In another moment Little Raven could see what it was doing. It was going around the cave room, peering by the light of the candle onto all of the shelves. Soon it would go around the room completely and would come, at last, to the shelf by the entrance from the river.

That would be the end of the story of Little Raven and the Red Coat who lived beyond Turtle Mountain. All that the hidden Indian lad could see of the creature was its lower limbs. At first, across the cave, he could only make out that it was a man, not an animal of four legs. As it drew nearer

127

to him, he could see the heavy fur-lined leggings and the high winter moccasins that the man wore. Indeed, he could see them very well. For they had stopped just outside of his hiding place and were no more than an arm's reach away from him.

It was then that Little Raven acted without thinking. While the man was searching the shelf immediately over him, Little Raven drew the rusted firewood axe of Cheyenne Man from his belt. Without hesitation and just as the fur-clad giant was about to shine the candle into his dark retreat, Little Raven struck with all his force at the big toe of the moccasin right in front of him.

He did not miss, and it was exactly the same toe he had struck before on the trail to Turtle Mountain. As Knife Eye screamed in agony and once more grasped the wounded toe, he dropped his candle, and its flame went out. In that instant of welcome darkness, Little Raven rushed past the medicine man, dived into the outer passageway, raced for his freedom along its rocky throat.

He won the race, too. Bursting forth into the fresh air and sunshine of the riverbank, where the cavern's secret exit lay screened by a huge fallen log and some alder brush, the Mandan boy wanted to shout his joy and gladness to be free. Yet he did not dare. It was still possible that Knife Eye would not know it was he who had been in his lodge and his treasure caves. The floors were very hard and would show no footprint of such a small boy. The ponies could not talk and neither could the sled dogs. Perhaps if Little Raven ran as swiftly as the snowshoe hare, and never looked back at the riverbank cavern entrance, then the medicine man would think someone else had been there.

If he, Little Raven, could just crawl up on top of that huge fallen log that hid the cave's entrance, he could run along its length without leaving any tracks. There was no snow on top of the old giant of the forest. By its friendly path, he could reach the river's hard ice, where his footprints would also leave no message. *Ih!* Cheyenne Man had been right. It never paid to give up. One always had to *try.*

Little Raven did try. He leaped and scrambled to the top of the log, ran along it to the river ice, and by the ice, swift as the wind, to the edge of the forest far up the stream. There he hid among the willows and lay still as a newborn fawn, watching back toward the entrance of the secret caverns of the Assiniboin medicine man.

He had not long to wait. Very soon, the dark head and shoulders of Knife Eye protruded from the mouth of the passageway. Little Raven could see him very clearly in the late afternoon sunshine. The medicine man's face was drawn in angry lines. His mouth was thin and narrow as a knife cut. His eyes seemed on fire with the fierce rage burning inside his heart.

But it was when the hidden Mandan boy looked toward the hands of the medicine man to see if he had the deadly black rifle with him that he saw something even more menacing than the gun. Knife Eye was holding the hunting bow of Little Raven's uncle in his hands.

Even as he now glared out of the cave, scanning the river ice and forest snow for some sign of the vanished visitor to his sacred home, he looked down at the bow and nodded his head. Then he withdrew again into the cave, and was gone.

But Little Raven knew what that last nod had meant. Knife Eye knew the markings on that bow. Every Mandan put his mark on his weapons, using his own personal color of paint and his own sign of ownership. The medicine man had read the sign on the bow that Little Raven had forgotten and left behind him in the second cavern. That was why he had nodded so grimly. Knife Eye would know, now, who had been his guest and who knew *all* of his secrets.

Eighteen

~

Little Raven did not know in what manner the medicine man would set upon the hunt for him. Neither could he wait to discover that way. He had his food for the mother wolf and for his journey to Turtle Mountain. Also, even as Cheyenne Man had predicted, the blizzard was threatening to return in earnest now. The sky was growing dark, the wind beginning to moan once more. He would need to hurry were he to reach his wolf friends before the deep snows flew to block the trails. Taking a last look toward Knife Eye's secret cave, the Mandan boy turned to go. It was then that he realized for the first time that he had left more than his uncle's bow behind him in the lair of Knife Eye.

His snowshoes! He had left them upon the shelf above the lodge's entrance tunnel! Any last doubt about the grave danger he faced was gone from the brave boy's breast. What was he to do? Fortunately it appeared as though the gods had given him a little time in which to think. He could still see no sign of Knife Eye, either at the cave's entrance or at the lodge's exit. Nothing stirred over there. Even the six ferocious sled dogs seemed fast asleep in their beds of snow.

Good. Praise the gods that were kind to little boys. During the day the sun had melted a bit of the top of the snow. In the past hour, with the great cold of the blizzard's breath blowing again, a hardening crust was forming upon the snow. Within a few minutes a boy of light weight, such as Little Raven, might run quickly over this new crust. He might, with luck, reach the village and report to the chief, Black Cat, what he had seen in the caves of Knife Eye. In such case, he would be saving his own life, but at the price of the mother wolf's. For it was as certain as the sunset that the chief and his new father, Cheyenne Man, would never permit an eleven-year-old boy to venture forth into the teeth of the second blizzard. Nor would they, or any of the other Mandans, offer to take the food to the mother wolf. So it became quite simple again. Little Raven could save his own life or risk that same life to save the mother wolf and her little ones. The Indian youth was vastly sobered by this knowledge, but he did not hesitate with the choice. He had made that long ago.

Once more he turned to go. He planned to travel up Mother Missouri on her hard ice where he would need no snowshoes. Then he would take the tributary stream that ran near the wolf den, following its frozen surface until he came to his journey's end close by the den. By that time the forest snows would be crusted enough to bear his small weight. All would yet end well, he told himself. But he was still Indian enough to cover the optimism with one more cautious glance back at the lodge of Knife Eye.

He was almost sorry he had looked, and certainly very frightened. Knife Eye was coming out of the lodge. He had the black rifle with him. The sled dogs, led by yellow-eyed Chaka, were greeting their master with wolfish howls and snarlings. They seemed eager for the chase. The blizzard wind, blowing from the direction of the lodge, brought to the hidden Mandan boy the muffled sounds of the medicine man speaking to his team. The words were not clear, but the tone of them was. Little Raven shuddered with the thought.

Over at the medicine lodge, Knife Eye was doing a sinister thing. While he had hooked five of the dogs to the sled, he had not harnessed great Chaka, the leader. He had Chaka on a chain that he held in his hand. Even as Little Raven watched from up the river, the medicine man spoke to the lead dog, and the brute cried out in its deep voice, lunging away through the snow. Knife Eye came after him. After Knife Eye came the team with the sled. All of them bore directly toward the river and the secret entrance to the caverns, and Little Raven realized why. At the mouth of the entrance, Knife Eye would set Chaka upon Little Raven's trail. The boy's fear mounted unbearably.

Where the eyes of the medicine man could not follow his footprints, the nose of the sled dog could read those footprints as plainly as though they were stamped in red war paint. Chaka would unravel his trail down the top of the big log and out onto the river ice. After that, it would be over very quickly. For no man, much less any small boy, could hope to outrun a sled dog on hard ice.

Little Raven very nearly gave up then. Yet the words of Cheyenne Man came to him again. *It is never too late to try.*

It was true that Chaka would need some time to figure out the scent line from the cave entrance to the log's top. Whatever that time might be, Little Raven now resolved to use as best he might, and he had one friend coming to his aid.

Overhead and through the thicket where he lay, the wind of the blizzard was searching with icy fingers ever more insistent. The daylight was completely gone. The river stretched dark and forbidding to the north. The air was filling with big flakes announcing the great storm to follow. In the time it required to tighten the belt of his wolf-skin coat and to pull its warm hood forward, Little Raven found the flakes so thick he knew that neither Knife Eye nor Chaka could see him leave his hiding place.

With a last prayer to whatever gods were still watching over him, Little Raven left his hiding place in the willows and set off up the frozen road of the big river. Behind him, even through the increasing cry of the blizzard's wind, he heard another sound that put the swiftness of the owls wings upon his fearful heels. It was the eerie howling of the great wolf dog, Chaka, coming upon the beginnings of Little Raven's track line at the mouth of the river cave's entrance.

Nineteen

Little Raven went up the big river with his back hunched to the rising wind of the blizzard. He found and followed the small side stream that led from the Missouri to the wolf's den. In the shelter of the great pines the force of the wind was lessened. He could hear more plainly than out on the great open sweep of the Missouri. Of a sudden, he thought he heard the approach of a dreaded sound behind him. To make sure, he stopped and cupped his hand to his ear. It might have been only some trick of the Blizzard Giant's voice that fooled him. He must remain calm. Only women and children became uncertain with nerves from such things. Little Raven was beginning to believe that he was almost a warrior grown, even at his age.

But it was not the Blizzard Giant playing tricks upon him. No wind ever barked and cried in that particular savage tone. Those were the sounds of Chaka, the sled-dog leader, drawing near behind him!

Then, in a moment when the wind died away even more completely, another sound came to the straining ears of the small Indian boy. It was the hoarse, deep voice of Knife Eye urging on his fierce companion to race even more swiftly along the track line of Little Raven.

There was only one thing for the Indian youth to do.

That was to keep on and never to give up. An ordinary Mandan boy might have surrendered then. Not Little Raven, the foster son of Cheyenne Man. In Little Raven's veins flowed the proud blood of Sacajawea, Canoe Woman who had led the American captains Lewis and Clark to the great western sea where the sun slept. The thought of this heritage, which made of him more than a mere Mandan, now returned to Little Raven and with it the determination to go on. He remembered Cheyenne Man's saying he must always be proud of his mixed blood. He must never forget that it made him stronger than others, not weaker or inferior in any way. He must recall the glories that were Canoe Woman's and Shahaka's and great black York's. Doing so, he must never fail to make the final attempt, no matter how dark the light of hope ahead.

So now the Mandan boy struggled onward through ever-deepening snows. Behind him came the sounds of Chaka and Knife Eye. Always nearer came those sounds. Soon they were so close that Little Raven could dimly see the forms of the big dog and the gaunt medicine man coming on his heels. Indeed, they grew so near to the fleeing boy that Knife Eye began to fire at him with his rifle. One bullet clipped a pine branch squarely in front of his face, showering him with bits of wood and snow. Another bullet struck the snow between his flying feet. A third bullet cut the fur of his coat's hood, passing only inches from striking him in the head. Little Raven believed that the end was but a matter of a few more struggling steps.

But in the last instant, he spied a tiny rivulet of ice that entered the creek he was following. He turned aside on the icy rivulet and hid beneath a spruce tree's spreading boughs. A gust of wind swirled up the outer creek, creating a cloud of snow that for the moment blinded the sight of

Chaka and Knife Eye. In the same moment, the snow swirl covered over the footprints of Little Raven, confusing the sharp nose of Chaka. The great dog went whiningly past the hiding place of Little Raven, searching the main creeklet beyond for that spot where the fleeing boy's footprints might be scented once more. With the dog, cursing the animal for losing the track line, went Knife Eye.

Waiting only until the snowflakes blotted out the forms of the man and the dog, Little Raven left his hiding place. The small rivulet led in the direction of the mother wolf's den, and he followed it quickly away from the main creeklet and from Chaka and Knife Eye.

In a very short time he was at the place of the wolf den. Or rather he was at the place where the wolf den *ought* to have been. But it was not there. It had vanished.

Twenty

~

It was a bad feeling to think one knew where he was, only to discover suddenly that he did not. Little Raven's heart had barely skipped a beat when he saw a pale yellow spot in the snowbank directly in front of him. Ah! That was better. He now understood what had happened while he was away. The old snow had been blown over the entrance to the den. The pale yellow stain in the drift was the sign of the breathing of the animals within.

Swiftly the Mandan youth dug into the bank. *Ah hai!* It was the right place! Soon he found himself in the familiar tunnel leading to the denning room. But when he had reached the rear cave where the she-wolf had her whelps, he sensed something wrong. It was too quiet. There was no warning growl from the mother wolf, no whine of greeting when she had his friendly scent. Neither were there any whimperings from the babies.

Little Raven found the nesting place where the wolf cubs had been. There were no babies in it. There was not even any warmth remaining from their little bodies. He called out to the mother wolf, but received no answer. The den was deserted. While he had gone seeking food for her, the mother wolf had moved her family. The Indian boy understood why. It was because he had found the den. He re-

membered now that a wolf will always move its whelps once
their birth place has been discovered by man. Little Raven's
feeling of debt to the mother wolf suddenly changed to a
sense of guiltiness for forcing the poor creature to leave her
warm home.

As weak from hunger as she was, the mother wolf had in
some manner summoned the strength to carry all of her
young ones to some other hiding place. Now Little Raven
would never see her or the whelps again. All of his danger
and woe in bringing to them the food stolen from Knife Eye
was a wasted thing. More than that. If death now came to
the little family, it would be the fault of Little Raven. It was
he who had driven them out into the storm.

As this bad thought overcame him, the Mandan youth
took new alarm. He heard the sound of the nails of some
large animal scraping upon sand and dirt. The sound was
not coming from the cave's entrance in the rivulet's bank
but from the opposite side of the denning room where he
now crouched. More remembrances of the ways of the wolf
came flooding into Little Raven's mind.

The wolf, not the owl or the fox, was the wisest of the
animals. Any Indian knew this. The wolf, for one thing, always made certain that it had "two ways to go", as the
hunters said. As to their dens, this meant that each place
they chose to make their home must have a rear as well as a
front entrance. It was from this rear entrance that the sound
of animal paws was now nearing.

Could it be the mother wolf returning? No, what would
she want in the empty den? Was there a father wolf? A
savage big male who would not understand that Little
Raven was the friend of his family?

The Indian lad shrank back against the cave's farther
wall. He took from his inner belt the rusted axe of Chey-

enne Man. If he must die, let it be as a warrior fighting to the last. Yet he knew it would not be much of a fight. If that was a bear squeezing down that rear entrance hole, or a panther, or even a big lynx—not to mention the father wolf—then the last battle of Little Raven would be a very brief clash indeed.

It was a frightening moment. Then two slanted green eyes were staring at him from the rear hole. They were leaving the hole and moving toward him. They were almost in his face, and he was too paralyzed with fear to raise the axe. He was helpless.

It was in this moment that the green eyes blinked, and Little Raven heard the familiar greeting whine of his friend, the she-wolf.

"Mother Wolf!" he cried out. "Welcome to your home! I am very happy it is you, believe me!"

The she-wolf growled deeply in her throat. It was a troubled sound. Little Raven crawled to her side. She was lying down and whimpering in the manner of a dog that has injured itself and requires the help of a human being. Little Raven stroked her weary head and spoke words of courage to her.

As his eyes were now becoming used to the den's darkness, he could see that his friend was exhausted by her efforts to carry her little ones away. She had strained herself too far. Now she did not seem able to stand any longer, or to walk. All she could do was to lie upon her side, pant slowly, and whine pleadingly for Little Raven to aid her. This he did not believe he could do. Except, of course, that he might feed her some of the meat he had brought, if she were not too weak to eat it.

"Here, Mother Wolf," he said, holding forth for her a choice morsel of the buffalo meat. "Please see if you have the strength to chew upon this small piece of tenderloin fat. It will help you."

The she-wolf had barely enough energy to open her jaws. Yet, encouraged by the Indian boy, she did get the meat between her teeth and did chew and swallow it. When Little Raven had thus fed her several mouthfuls of the tender meat and fat, he could literally see the life and strength coming back into her body. By the time that she had taken every scrap of the meat, she was recovered enough to sit up on her haunches and to lick the boy's face in gratitude.

In return, he patted her gently and placed his arms about the thick fur of her neck. She growled and snuggled closer to him.

"Mother Wolf," he told her, "you had better hurry back to your babies now. You have new strength to travel, and new milk to give to them from the buffalo meat you have eaten just now. I will go to my home and bring still more meat for you, for I know where a great deal of it is stored. We will meet in this old den, and I shall feed you again." He paused to squeeze her tightly and pat her big head. "Let us be brave," he said. "When I tell my new father and my tribe's chief about Knife Eye and all that stored meat, my people will want to reward you. You see, you saved my life. This made it possible for me to save their lives. They will understand. You and your babies will have food and will never be hunted or harmed by any Mandan Indian of the band of Black Cat in this land. All right, mother?"

But the wolf only whimpered again. She was not reassured by the boy's words. Something was disturbing her. She bumped at Little Raven with her nose. She took the sleeve of his coat in her teeth and tugged upon it. It seemed to him as if she were trying to lead him, to urge him to move. He got up and allowed her to guide him. She led the way across the den and came to a place behind a gnarled tree root that grew down into the den from above. As she did this, Little Raven heard an answering wolf noise that never was uttered by an adult animal, mother or father.

Then he knew. There was still one of the cubs remaining in the den. Evidently the little thing had become caught under the twisted root, or the mother had hidden it there against her return. Probably it was both things. The mother had put her baby in under the root, then could not get it out again.

Little Raven felt beneath the root. Yes, he was right. The baby was caught. But Little Raven said a quick prayer to his Indian gods. At last he could do something to repay the mother wolf. Working swiftly, but with delicate care not to strike the tiny cub, he chopped away the root with his rusted axe. He had the baby freed in a very short time and handed it up to the mother.

Happily the she-wolf licked and examined the baby. Deciding it had not been harmed, she picked it up in her jaws and started toward the rear entrance to the den. There she stopped. After a moment of soft whining, she put the baby down upon the ground and peered up and out along the tunnel.

Going to her side, Little Raven joined her. There was some light in that rear tunnel. It was a short tunnel and had recently been opened by the mother wolf on her return. Yet, even as the Indian youth and the starving she-wolf lay side-by-side looking out of the den, Little Raven could see that the hole was filling up rapidly. He could hear as well as see the reason for this. The new blizzard had grown in its fury. Now it raged in full terror above them. The sight and sound of its icy rage was enough to give pause to any beast, even the she-wolf, and to any boy, even a Mandan descendent of Sacajawea, Shahaka, and York.

"What is it, Mother Wolf?" whispered the lad. "Do you fear to take the baby with you in such a storm?"

She thumped the earthen floor of the cave with her tail.

"Ah," the boy said, "so that is it. You are saying to yourself . . . 'Now, what shall I do? I have already moved the other babies, and it is a long way to the new home that I must carry this last one. See how the wind has grown colder and wilder in its anger. I shall never make it safely back to the other babies carrying this baby which whimpers to me here. But if I go on, swiftly now, leaving this one baby here, then I will be able to come to the new den and feed the other babies. What a cruel thing for a mother to decide!' "

Little Raven gave the mother wolf another hug. "Listen, is that what you think, mother?" he asked her.

Again, whether she understood his words or only the gentle tone of his voice, the she-wolf whined hopefully.

"I thought so." The Indian youth nodded. "Now then, listen to me very carefully. Is there anything I may do for you? Is there any way in which I can aid you? Answer me if you can. Show me what it is."

As he said this last thing, her soft growl changed to a different level. She looked long at Little Raven. There was pain in her beautiful green eyes. But there was also in those eyes a positive expression of faith and great relief. She arose from her position by his side and once more took up the tiny cub in her jaws.

Then she did a strange thing, and, in a way, a most trusting and wonderful thing. She did not go out of the rear tunnel with the little wolf. She brought it, instead, to where Little Raven sat by the entrance way. There, without another sound, she gently dropped the tiny cub into the lap of the Indian boy. She gave it a final soft nuzzling with her moist nose, then once more licked Little Raven on the cheek. With that, she turned and crawled out of the den through the rear tunnel way, and was gone.

The Mandan boy called after her excitedly. He said to her that she must return. That she had forgotten her little baby. That she must not leave it to die alone. But Little Raven knew that the mother wolf would not answer him and would never return. He knew, as well, that she had not forgotten her baby, or left it in that den to die. Understanding in her poor brute's mind that she might fail in reaching her other babies with this final one borne in her tired jaws, she had decided to entrust its precious life to an Indian boy who wore a wolf-skin coat and who had said to her that he was her friend.

There was no other explanation for it, no other way for Little Raven to think of it. The savage mother had surrendered her last whelp. She had given it to Little Raven. This last little wolf was his.

Twenty-One

The wolf cub whimpered and nestled closer into the wolf-skin coat of Little Raven. Perhaps it thought the coat was its mother's fur. Also it was looking for its supper. The boy could feel its small nose bumping at his chest. Then, when the cub found not warm milk but only skinny Mandan bones and dark skin, it commenced to cry louder than before.

Little Raven held it closer, trying to think what to do. The answers were not easy. They could not stay in the wolf den through this second storm. There was no mother's milk to sustain them. Even though Little Raven was tough and wiry, as small boys are, and even though he might thus go without food for a long time, the baby wolf could not. It must be fed, and soon. But how?

Already the small thing was nursing at the Indian boy's fingers. It was growling angrily, too, for no milk came to reward its fierce little tuggings. Little Raven had to laugh at the tiny creature's temper. "Do not devour my fingers," he pleaded. "I have only ten of them and am fond of each one."

Yet his reassuring words settled nothing. There was the decision to be made. Brave laughing would fill no small wolf's belly. Steady words calmed the nerves but would not substitute for mother's milk. Quickly the Mandan boy decided his course.

It was to go and seek out Black Cat, the chief. He would tell the stern leader of his band everything. Then Black Cat might do as he thought honorable and fair to all. If he believed he should punish Little Raven, very well. If he believed Knife Eye should be sent into the snow to starve—the tribal law for those who hoarded food in time of famine—then that, too, was all right. If the chief, likewise, believed Cheyenne Man should decide the penalty for Little Raven, this would be just, also. Even if the chief did not choose to believe Little Raven's story of the caverns beneath the medicine man's lodge, or was fearful of going to that lodge to learn the real truth, Little Raven would have to accept his judgment, and he would do so.

There was but one exception the Mandan boy made. If Black Cat, or Cheyenne Man, or a single one of the Mandan band of his people sought to harm the little wolf, then that was not all right. Little Raven would fight then. Little Raven had been given the trust of that small life by the tiny beast's mother. He would guard that trust with his own life if need be. Indian honor could demand no less.

Swiftly the boy prepared to go back out into the blizzard. He knew the dangers out there. The wind was even wilder than that of the previous storm. The snow was falling even more thickly. Yet, if he waited for it to stop, the cub would perish. If he went out into it, he himself might perish. Even if they went out in it and the storm eased to make their safe return to the village more possible, then that very easement would also make it more possible for Knife Eye and Chaka to see them and to shoot them down with the black rifle.

Little Raven told himself that he was not afraid. After all, had he not found his way back to the village in one storm? Was there any good reason he could not do so in another storm, even a bigger one? No. The real problem was to keep a keen eye out for the medicine man and the savage sled dog, Chaka. The Blizzard Giant was a kind friend by comparison to these two other enemies. They, and the long black rifle.

"Come on, little brother," the Mandan boy murmured determinedly. "We are going home."

He placed the cub in the fur hood of his parka. The small whelp fitted very snugly in the new nest. Little Raven pulled tight the drawstring of the hood, making the baby even more secure against the wind and snow. Only the small animal's nose protruded from the shelter of the parka's hood. Little Raven made a final adjustment, setting the hood so that it hung exactly between his thin shoulder blades.

Looking back over his shoulder, he said to the cub: "Are you all right in there?"

It was a very wise little cub and did not struggle or cry when he spoke. It just wiggled its stumpy tail and panted happily.

"Be very quiet, then," said the boy. "Chaka could hear one of your thin yelps for a long way, even in this wind."

With the advice, he bent down and crawled on all fours out of the front entrance tunnel to the small frozen brook that ran outside it. *Good,* he announced to himself, glancing up and down the stream. *The wind and snow have lessened just enough. We have only to follow this rivulet to the larger one, and down it to Mother Missouri and our village. We shall be home in a very few miles, small wolf friend. Trust your new brother, Little Raven.*

The cub stuck its nose out of the hood. It licked the snowflakes that stuck to that nose. In the back pack of the parka, Little Raven could feel its small body move once more against his own and knew that the stumpy tail was wiggling again.

"That's right, wolf brother." The boy smiled. "You will see. Everything is going to be fine for both of us. The gods are watching out for their two children."

The cub panted eagerly, small eyes shining. Little Raven bent forward, leaning into the force of the wind. Down the rivulet he went. There was only enough new snow on the ice of the stream to make good footing. The lack of his snowshoes was unimportant, praise the gods.

On he went, out upon the surface of the larger creek, on down it toward the big river. All seemed well. There was not the least sign of Knife Eye or fierce Chaka. Both the wind and snow of the blizzard had retreated a little. Even the cold was less severe. *Ih,* how kind of the gods! It was time, thought the grateful Little Raven, to turn his face skyward and say some of the prayer words of the Mandan people.

The boy began to do this. But he did not get to finish his prayer. All at once the wind began to blow again. It was as if the Blizzard Giant had been waiting only to lure the Indian youth out of the warm wolf's den onto the frigid river ice before pouncing treacherously upon him. The snow returned with a fury such as Little Raven had never seen. He had no real chance against it. It swirled and whirled and blasted out of the northland as one great icy cloud. In a few moments, the boy could not see his own hand extended before his face.

He attempted to turn back and follow the creek to the wolf den but could not see the stream's ice now, nor could he feel it, so swiftly had the new snow covered it over. Turning to go the other way, on toward Mother Missouri, he knew the final fear. He could not see his own tracks any more. The snow filled them even as his moccasins made them. Little Raven had no way to turn then. He was lost. Lost in a blue-cold winter's blizzard sweeping him away toward the icy Land of the Grandmother. Lost without food. Lost with no wood for a fire. Lost even without any shelter from the slashing teeth of the Arctic wind.

For himself, Little Raven understood the truth. He was a Mandan. He knew what this white blindness meant. The Great Spirit of his people had forgotten his two children in the storm. He was no longer watching over them. Another Indian god had come to stand in his place. This other god was called the Dark One. He was the Mandan god who guarded the gateway to the Land of the Shadows, the same one who had been in the lodge of his uncle while Little Raven sat in the council of elders with Cheyenne Man.

The white men had another name for this god. They called him Death.

Twenty-Two

Little Raven realized he could not stay where he was. If he took shelter in a snow bank, he would drowse off and not awaken again. The thing he must do was drift with the wind. He must put his back to the blizzard and permit it to blow him where it might. The Indian traveler never fought the icy blast. So now the Mandan youth "followed the wind".

On and on he went. The snow became deeper, the air colder. His hands and feet were soon so cold he could not feel them. Frost covered his face, especially where the moisture of his breathing collected near mouth and nostrils. Before long, he had little strength remaining. In some time he had not heard the baby wolf whimper, although he had taken the little beast from the parka's hood and placed it inside his wolf-skin coat near his heart. With his last willed power he forced his legs to take him toward a mound of snow that he could see dimly ahead of him. He had come into a stand of pine timber so that the flakes were not so heavy in the air or the wind so severe. He had noticed a dark space beneath the snow mound. He believed it to be the shadow of a shelter place beneath a large boulder that, in turn, had caused the snow mound to heap up above it. He did not remember reaching the snow mound or the shelter of the dark spot that it promised. He did remember falling heavily into the snow just before he got to the mound. There he lay helpless to arise again.

He thought what a sad thing it was that he could not go on with possible safety but a few steps beyond. He attempted to murmur some apology to the little wolf cub, but his lips were frozen together with ice. He was so stiff with the cold, indeed, that he could not even move his hand to place it within the wolf-skin coat and pat the cub. He thought he heard its faint whimper, however, and that comforted him somewhat.

He could feel himself becoming sleepy then. This he knew was the final sign. Yet he no longer had the will to fight on. He lay there, eyes closing, breath coming more calmly. After a brief prayer to the gods that they should shelter his people through the great cold, bringing them food by some miracle, and firewood, he did not open his eyes again.

The wind, as if in respect for him, tugged gently at the snow about the place where he fell, pulling it over him. The Blizzard Giant also slowed his howling, it seemed. The stillness in the pinewood was complete. Not even the wolf puppy whined, nor did it wiggle any more.

Little Raven, a small Indian boy, was asleep. The gods of his people had heard his prayer. They did not disturb him where he lay. They only commanded the great storm to hold its breath in honor of his bravery.

Twenty-Three

Little Raven did not sleep forever. After a time, he opened his eyes and found himself in a wonderful place. It was warm, and there was no wind. It was lighted by a cheery yellow glow. He was lying upon a wooden bed with a beautiful Hudson's Bay blanket spread over him and a soft buffalo robe beneath him. The blanket was of the kind traded by the Turtle Mountain post to the Canadian Indians. But this was no Indian's house in which the Mandan boy found himself. It was a white man's house, such a small emergency shelter hut of sapling logs as the white fur trappers built in the north woods. Little Raven could scarcely believe his good fortune to be in it, safe from the storm.

He sat up on the bed, rubbing his eyes and saying aloud some few words of thanks to the gods. As he did this, a man's deep voice spoke to him in Mandan, his own tongue. "Well," said the voice, "I should think you would save some small gratitude for me. After all, I saw no gods about when I found you in the snow and brought you inside."

Little Raven turned unblinkingly toward the fireplace. There, leaning upon the mantelpiece, a kindly smile on his face, stood the tallest man he had ever seen. He was as big, almost, as Knife Eye. The white man was smoking a pipe and grinning at Little Raven. The Indian boy believed the

big white man had the bluest eyes and the friendliest smile
of all men. He touched his small hand to his forehead in the
Indian gesture of deepest respect.

"Thank you for saving me from the cold," he said slowly.
"I cannot pay you, for I am poor. My name is Little Raven.
As you have guessed, I am a Mandan. Well, almost a
Mandan."

The big white man nodded, frowning a bit. "Why do you
say 'almost'?" he asked.

Little Raven told him the story of his relationship with
Sacajawea and the black slave of Lewis and Clark, the great
African Negro, York. The white man nodded again.

"That's proud blood," he said gravely. "No wonder you
are so tough and did not die out there in the cold."

Little Raven shook his head sadly. His memory was
coming back to him now. He was thinking of why he had
been out in that cold and how he had failed in his purpose.
"I am not tough enough," he told the white man. "Now my
people will starve and it is they who will die."

"Oh, well, how is that?" asked the tall man. "Has the
bad winter used up all of their meat? All of their wood?"

"Yes. They have a few scraps of stringy pony meat remaining to them all, and a few sticks of burning wood."

The white man came over to the bed. He sat down upon
its side and put his hand on the Indian boy's shoulder.
"Which Mandans are these?" he asked.

"The band of Black Cat. Our village is near where
Mother Missouri turns toward the west."

"I know the place," said his companion. "It is not very
far from where we are. But you have still come a long way
through the blizzard for such a small boy."

"Yes, I tried hard."

"You're a brave boy. Now go back to sleep and regain

153

your strength. I will fix you some warm food. We can eat when you awaken. Are you warm enough with just that blanket over you?" Without waiting for Little Raven's reply, the big man reached toward a nearby chair. "Here," he said, taking a garment from the back of the chair, "let me put my coat over you as well."

Little Raven nodded gratefully, and lay back upon the bed. But as the tall man was placing the coat over him, he came bolt upright again.

"Is that *your* coat?" he exclaimed, looking in awe at the brilliant garment the man had removed from the chair. "Do you really wear this coat of scarlet?"

"Why, yes." The man laughed. "Why do you ask? Do you think that I stole it?"

Little Raven could not believe what he saw or what he heard. He shook his head wonderingly. "*You* are a Red Coat?" he asked. "A *real* Red Coat?"

Again the tall white man laughed. "Yes," he said. "I am a real Red Coat. My name is Sergeant Mackenzie."

"Sar-jen Ma-Kahn-zy?" murmured Little Raven, the white man's name falling oddly from his Indian tongue.

"Yes, but I think you better call me Red Coat. That's a good Indian name, eh?"

"Yes." The boy nodded soberly. "That is what the Mandans call your tribe. Thank you, Red Coat." He looked around the trapper's little shack once more. "Is this your house?" he asked. "Do you live here all of the time?"

"No, this is just some trapper's cabin. I took shelter in it from the storm. I was only passing this way searching for a bad man."

"Did you find him, Red Coat?"

"Not yet. He is very clever."

"He is a white man, this bad one?"

"No, I am sorry to say, he is an Indian."

"Not a Mandan?"

"I don't know, Little Raven. The mounted police know only that he sells whisky to the other Indians."

"Oh, I thought only white men did that . . . selling whisky to the Indians, I mean. Are you sure it is not a white . . . ?" As he began to ask the question, a great excitement came into the mind of Little Raven. "Wait!" he cried out. "I know of an Indian who keeps whisky in his secret caves beneath his lodge. Do you think he might be the one?"

The mounted policeman did not show the same excitement as the Mandan boy. He had followed many stories of many whisky sellers in the long search for this bad Indian they now spoke of. Still, this was an unusual little boy.

"Oh?" he said, pausing to light his pipe again. "What Indian is that?"

"His name is Knife Eye. He is a medicine man who lives near my village on Mother Missouri."

"Ah," said Sergeant Mackenzie slowly. "We know of him. He is a Canadian Assiniboin, a bad man, all right. But how do you know he sells whisky?"

Little Raven then quickly told his story to the tall man. He left out nothing, nor did he seek to protect this own dishonor in running away, stealing meat, telling the lie to his new father, or a solitary word of what he had tried to do in saving the Mandan people from starving in the cold.

At the end, telling of the mother wolf, he spoke sadly. "So," he said, "I took the last little baby wolf, which she gave to me. I put the tiny creature in my parka hood and set out through the blizzard. It grew colder, and I put him inside my coat. We went on and on. I saw the dark spot in the snow ahead of us. I tried to reach it but did not. The last

155

thing that I remember was the whining inside my coat of the little wolf. Then I stumbled and. . . ." The Indian youth broke off his story, his face showing great remorse. "The baby wolf," he said, "must even now lie dead of the great cold out there in the snow. What a sorrowful thing."

The tears sprang to the eyes of the boy and coursed down his dark cheeks. Sergeant Mackenzie only smiled once more and dried the tears with his big hand and the corner of the Hudson's Bay blanket.

"Don't cry," he said gently. "Come over here by the fire and look into the wood box. I want to show you something."

Little Raven obeyed him, even though his heart was sad. He came to the wood box and glanced down into it. Then his heart nearly leaped from his throat. There in the box, curled up warmly as a snowy mitten set to dry by a lodge fire, lay the tiny wolf cub.

Little Raven dropped to his knees beside the box. He touched the puppy with careful fingers, not awakening him.

"That is good," said the white man. "Don't disturb him. He saved your life, you know."

"What?" said Little Raven, surprised. "This tiny thing saved *me?*"

"Yes. The dark spot you were trying to reach in the snow was the wood pile of this cabin. When I went out to bring in some more wood for the fire, I heard the puppy crying. It's amazing how much noise a cold and hungry little pup of his age can make. He was really yipping, believe me!"

Little Raven shook his dark head. "It is very strange," he said, "that a wolf cub would save an Indian boy."

The tall white man looked at the Mandan youth questioningly. "Why do you keep calling him a wolf cub?" he asked.

"Because that is what he is," maintained Little Raven. "I found him in a wolf den and his mother was a wolf. What more proof does one need?"

"Proof of his father." His big companion smiled. "This pup is not a wolf, Little Raven. Look more closely at him."

Bending down, the man lifted the sleeping cub and placed him in the Indian boy's hands. "Study him carefully," he told Little Raven. "Hold him up to the fire's light."

Little Raven did so. He had never seen the cub in a good light before. First the darkness of the den, then the darkness of the storm, had prevented him examining his gift from the mother wolf. Now, staring at the tiny beast, his bright eyes snapped with returning excitement.

"Why!" he said quickly, "you are right, Red Coat. He has four white paws and a curly black coat, with a large white star on his breast. I never saw a wolf of that marking."

"What has happened," explained the big mounted policeman, "is that the father was a dog and the mother a wolf. This is not uncommon, as you know. A great many of the best sled dogs in this north country are partly of wolf blood."

"Yes, yes," said Little Raven, "I have heard that from my people. Ah, how glad I am that this is true. Now I can return to my village with this little one and Black Cat will not make me put him into the band's boiling pot."

"We shall see that no harm comes to him," promised the other. "Get back into the bed, now, Little Raven. You have to rest up for the journey."

"The journey, Red Coat?"

"Of course. Did you think I wouldn't help you get back to your village? You and your little dog?"

Little Raven smiled and made the apology sign of his

people. "I forgot," he murmured. "You are a Red Coat and they always help people."

"*Good* people," said the big man. "Now, into bed with you and no more talk."

Little Raven obeyed him. But as the blanket was being tucked in about him, his mind thought of something else. "But, Red Coat," he pleaded with sudden fear, "I cannot return to my village! The people have no food. First I must reach Turtle Mountain where the trading post is. My father, Cheyenne Man, told me they had food there. That the Red Coats lived near there and would save us if they could."

"Go on and sleep," said the tall, blue-eyed white man. "I am the only Red Coat from any place near Turtle Mountain, and I will help your people if I can. But first I must do my own duty."

Little Raven nodded, and lay back drowsily. "What duty is that, Red Coat?" he asked.

"To find the bad Indian who sells the whisky to your people," answered the mounted policeman.

"Do you mean Knife Eye, the Assiniboin?"

"If that is his name and his tribe, then, yes."

"I will help you," vowed the Mandan boy. "I can guide you to the. . . ."

Even as he nodded with the promise, Little Raven fell fast asleep, his vow unfinished. His dreams were all good dreams, and contented. It was as though he knew that in that warm log cabin in the friendly pine woods, with the tall mounted policeman in the scarlet-red coat guarding his slumber, nothing at all of the vast north country could harm him—not even the evil Assiniboin medicine man.

Twenty-Four

~

When Little Raven awoke once more, his new friend, Red Coat, was no longer smiling.

"The storm is passing," said the mounted policeman. "We must travel now. Come, I have food ready."

They ate the good stew of pemmican and rabbit meat that Sergeant Mackenzie had cooked. When it was finished, Little Raven went to the one small window of the cabin and looked out. He shivered as he did.

"*Ih!*" he said. "It does not seem to me as though the storm were passing. We will freeze if we go out there. The snow will cover us up."

"Nevertheless," answered Sergeant Mackenzie, putting on his red coat, and then a big fur parka over it, "we must travel on. We have our duties to do."

Little Raven frowned. "*Our* duties?" he asked.

"Yes," answered the big policeman. "My duty is to find the bad Indian. Your duty is to show me where he stores the food, so that we may feed your people, and the whisky jugs, so that I may know if he is the Indian who sells the whisky."

Little Raven could see that this was just. "All right," he said, but then frowned again. "I just thought of something," he said. "Where is your pony? The Mandans say that the

Red Coats always ride horses."

"Not always," denied his friend. "You know a horse cannot go in such snow as this. We use snowshoes, even the same as you Indians. Come on, get into your coat."

"*Ih!*" said Little Raven again. "I just thought of something else. I have no snowshoes. I left them in the lodge of Knife Eye."

"I have an extra pair for you," nodded the other. "They belong to the trapper who lives here. We will borrow them, and I shall bring them back to him. Here they are."

He gave the large shoes to Little Raven.

"*Ih!*" cried the Mandan youth for the third time. "You will not believe it, Red Coat, but I have thought of yet another thing."

"Yes, what is that?"

"The little wolf dog. How about him?"

"Why, he must go, also, of course. I have fed him some mush and soft meat with warm water, and he is all ready to go. Put him in the inside of your coat. I would carry him, except that I must carry something else. Yes, and have my hands free to use it."

"What is that?" asked Little Raven, sensing the sternness in Sergeant Mackenzie's voice.

"You told me this medicine man had a fine black rifle, didn't you?" said the big man.

"Yes. It is like yours, hanging over the door, there. Only his is shinier and newer than yours."

"Never mind that," said his companion, taking the short-barreled rifle from its rack of deer antlers above the door. "These old carbines of ours seem to shoot straight enough."

This made Little Raven's eyes shine. "Yes," he said proudly. "I know that. My people say that the Red Coats never do miss their marks when they fire at them! They always hit the target in the center."

"Well,"—the tall policeman smiled—"they always *try* to."

"That is what my father, Cheyenne Man, says is most important of everything." The Mandan boy nodded. "Always to *try*."

"Very true," said Sergeant Mackenzie. "You have a good father, Little Raven. Listen to him carefully as you grow."

"I will, I promise you," said the boy.

"Good. Now get your puppy and come on. We have no time to spare."

They set out through the snow.

"Follow me closely," ordered the mounted policeman. "I know a forest trail where the wind is less cruel, the snow not so deep."

Little Raven only nodded and did as he was told. He had no breath for words. He needed all of it for working. The size of those big snowshoes of the trapper made the task of keeping up with the long-striding Red Coat very hard, indeed. But the Mandan boy did his best.

Sergeant Mackenzie watched him closely with his kind blue eyes. But he did it in a way that would make it appear that he was not worrying about his small companion.

After what seemed to the latter like all of the morning yet which was actually but an hour or so, the big policeman held up his glove and made the halting sign.

"We will take a rest here," he said. "I shall brew some tea, and we can eat a bit of pemmican to restore our strength. Also, I brought along something for the puppy."

"Thank you." Little Raven sighed, sinking down upon a log that lay nearby. "I do not really need a rest, but if you are weary, Red Coat, then I will wait for you."

"You are a good boy, very polite." His comrade nodded. "I think you will be a chief one day."

"I shall try to do better than Black Cat," said the boy.

"Don't blame your chief too much," advised the policeman. "Whisky is a strong enemy. It has ruined greater men than Black Cat."

"My new father, Cheyenne Man, is a great man," said Little Raven soberly. "He never drinks whisky."

"Be like him, then," said Sergeant Mackenzie, "and you will make a fine chief."

They stopped talking with that. Gathering some dry wood, they soon had a cheerful blaze crackling beside the log. In a few minutes the water for the tea had boiled, and they fell to eating their meal. In between bites, they sipped the hot, fragrant tea. Little Raven could feel its warmth spreading all the way to his numbed toes. It made his heart feel good. Adding to the pleasure, the gray clouds of the blizzard rolled away, allowing the sun to return and to shine brightly.

"Ah," said the Mandan boy, "isn't the sun beautiful, Red Coat? I always feel happy when the sun is shining at me."

Sergeant Mackenzie drained his cup. "Everything feels happy when the sun shines," he agreed. "The sun is the heartbeat of this world of ours. Without it all things would perish. All the men, all the animals, all the birds in the air and the fishes in the streams."

"*Ai, hai* . . . what a wondrous thing is the sun!" cried Little Raven.

"Indeed, it is," said the policeman, reaching for his pipe.

They sat quietly for a short time, warming their hands and stomachs at the fire, while the sun heated their backs. The wolf dog puppy was playing on a bed of pine needles that Little Raven had arranged for him. He had eaten his feeding of cornmeal mush and pemmican scraps that Sergeant Mackenzie had made for him in the trapper's cabin. It was difficult for such a young animal to eat the food, but with Little Raven's patient help, the puppy quickly learned. Now, watching him bite and growl at the pine needles, the Indian boy gave him the end of his first finger to chew upon, and to suck at. This he did fiercely, making both Little Raven and Sergeant Mackenzie laugh.

The policeman tamped the last of the tobacco firmly into the bowl and started looking for just the right ember from the fire to light up his pipe.

"You know, Little Raven," he said thoughtfully, "you must soon think of giving your puppy a name. What have you in mind? Some good Mandan word? The name of an animal? What?"

"Why, I don't know," admitted the boy, surprised. "To tell the truth, I had not thought about the matter. But you are surely right, Red Coat. What do you say his name should be? I think it must have pride and dignity, don't you?"

"By all means it must!" the white man agreed positively. He squinted his blue eyes at the strange-looking, curly-coated puppy. In all honesty, it was a very homely little animal. It was as small and dark and odd in its appearance as—well, as the little Mandan boy who now clutched the wriggling beast to his breast. The big policeman found the ember he wanted from the fire. He put its glowing heat to the tobacco in his pipe. "Well, now," he said, "let us see."

The ember went out in the cold before the pipe was lit, requiring that he poke in the fire for another.

"How about Ohhaw, because he appears so smart? Or Eapanopa to mean he will guard you when he grows up? Or perhaps Shahakohopinnee from the fact he has brought you good luck?"

Little Raven shook his head gravely. "He does not look like a Little Fox to me. Or like a Red Shield, either."

"Well, how about Shahakohopinnee, then?"

"Little Wolf's Medicine?" frowned the boy. "I must admit it's a good name. But it is too long. Besides, you have convinced me he is no wolf. I want a dog's name, Red Coat. Something that you feel to have the right sound."

Sergeant Mackenzie cocked his head to one side, studying the orphaned wolf dog of the forest. It was difficult for him to keep from smiling, so truly unlovely was the black runt of the she-wolf's litter. But he knew that he must never show doubt to the Mandan boy. This was no matter of humor to him.

"I have it!" the big policeman said at last. "It has just come to me as I observe his color and his noble bearing. Yes, and his look of toughness and strength. Did you ever notice an old smoke-darkened hunting boot?" he asked the boy. "One with the blackened soot and burned grease of many campfires soaked into it? That's a strong thing."

Little Raven did not seem convinced, somehow. "I don't know," he frowned impatiently. "An old hunting boot? Is that proud? Is that a thing of dignity?"

"Of course!" cried the policeman. "Say it in Mandan, Ompsehara, Black Moccasin. That's a beautiful name!"

"Yes, yes," agreed Little Raven, eyes shining. "I can see what you mean now. Oh, thank you, Red Coat."

"Don't thank me," said the big man hastily. "I only tried to do him justice. That's a beautiful dog you have there. He deserves a fine name."

Twenty-Five

They traveled onward through the forest land. Leaving it, they came into a more open country. Vast expanses of snow glared in the new sunlight. Sergeant Mackenzie stopped, and with his knife whittled out flat masks of willow bark. In these he cut slits for the eyes to peer through. Little Raven wore one of the masks, being told that in this way the blazing sun would not burn his eyes with snow blindness.

On they went. The Indian boy believed they must have snowshoed over ten miles. Sergeant Mackenzie could have told him it was less than half of that. As the sun began to sink a little to the west, the big policeman again made the halting sign.

"Will we camp here?" asked Little Raven hopefully.

"Ah, no," replied his companion. "We shall only rest again, as we did before. Don't tell me you are tired?"

Little Raven was so weary his whole body ached. "Never!" he said, and sank down upon a convenient stone.

Sergeant Mackenzie found another stone nearby. He got out his pipe and the tobacco. Loading the bowl, he lit it.

The first blue smoke, drifting away from his puffing to get the pipe going well, smelled very nice to Little Raven. The first smoke of lighted tobacco always had smelled in that good way to him. What a strange thing, he thought.

Tobacco smoke makes the lodge and the clothing and the breath stink, yet it makes the air smell delightful.

But he was not thinking mainly of tobacco smoke. "Red Coat," he said, when he had rested a bit, "I have been worrying about what waits for you near my village. How will it go when we arrive there?"

The big mounted policeman thought a moment. "Well," he said, puffing on his pipe, "to begin with, I shall need to be very careful. You see, Little Raven, we are not in Canada. Not in that country which you call the 'Land of the Grandmother'. Although it seemed to you like a far journey, struggling in such wind and snow, the trapper's cabin was an American trapper's cabin. We are far from my country of Canada, and far from even the Turtle Mountain trading post in your own land, toward which you vowed to travel."

"No!" objected Little Raven indignantly. "It cannot be so far to Turtle Mountain now. Why, I went a terrible distance through that storm!"

The sergeant shook his head, a small smile on his friendly, rough-hewn face. "Terrible it may have been," he said, "but a distance it was not. Do you know, Little Raven, that from where we sit on these rocks, it is over one hundred miles to the Turtle Mountain post? It is five days by easy pony ride in the summertime, or four days by good dog sled speed in the wintertime. Do you understand, now, why your good father, Cheyenne Man, did not try to reach Turtle Mountain himself? Neither he, nor any of the younger men, weak as they all are from the cold and hunger of this hard winter?"

"Yes," answered Little Raven in a humbled tone. "I was wrong to run away after I told Cheyenne Man I would not do so."

The Red Coat policeman studied him for several puffs of the pipe. Little Raven noticed how yellow his hair was in the sunlight, its color revealed when he had thrown back the hood of his parka to light his pipe. The Red Coat was certainly a fine sight, strong and fearless, with the sunshine in his hair.

"It's too soon to say how wrong you were to run away, Little Raven," the big policeman replied at last. "It depends upon what luck we have in finding this whisky seller of yours."

"We will find him, all right," assured the small Mandan youth. "I shall lead you squarely to his evil door." He hesitated, a frown crossing his face. "But that is what worries me," he said. "That is what I intended to ask you about."

Now it was his companion who frowned. "I do not understand what it is that worries you, boy," he said. "Try to say it in another way. Sometimes, you know, an Indian's tongue gets tangled talking with a white man. The same thing happens with the white man when he is talking with an Indian."

"Now I must ask what *you* mean?" Little Raven smiled, enjoying the exchange. "Is your tongue tangled right now, Red Coat?"

"Well,"—the tall policeman smiled back—"let us see . . . what I mean to tell you is that, while red man and white may speak one another's tongue, even as you and I, the meanings of the words sometimes get lost between us. This is to say that, while we may understand another man's tongue, we do not necessarily understand his heart. Does that make sense to you?"

Little Raven thought a moment. Then he nodded brightly. "Yes," he replied, "I believe that it does. You mean that we listen, but we do not always hear. Is that it, Red Coat?"

"That is exactly it," said the other. "You are wise beyond your winters, boy. That is why I am taking your story about the whisky seller seriously. That is why I am willing to come with you far from my own country, into yours. Even though there is an agreement of the law between my land of Canada and your land of America, I am going beyond the lines of my duty to arrest a man five pony rides into another country. Even a friendly country such as America. I'm not sure the Americans would be happy about it."

Again Little Raven furrowed his brow in puzzlement. "Why do you do it, then?" he asked. "I mean, why do you arrest Knife Eye? Why not just tell my people, the Mandans, what I have told you? Then show them the whisky and the food and all their furs in the caverns beneath the medicine lodge. If you did that, my people would take care of Knife Eye. You know, Red Coat, that hoarding food in a time of famine is a terrible crime among Indians. Worse, even, than killing another man. Or beating a child. Or showing cowardice in war. To hide food when others are starving . . . *ih!*"

"We are getting away from what worried you," the big man reminded him. "You haven't explained what it is that worries you about what will happen after we find the whisky seller."

"Oh," said the boy, "yes. Well, I was only wondering how you would capture Knife Eye, what you would do with him?"

The tall sergeant of the red-coated police nodded. He took a thoughtful puff on his pipe, blew the fragrant smoke outward. "I will simply put the handcuffs on him and take him as my prisoner to be tried by my people up in Canada."

"Hahndcufts?" echoed the Indian boy curiously.

Sergeant Mackenzie smiled and reached into his back pack. He brought out the handcuffs. They were gleaming circles of polished steel, with dazzling chains clinking between them.

"Beautiful!" exclaimed Little Raven delightedly. "How are they worn? Upon the arm above the elbows? About the throat as a necklace or breast ornament? Dangling from the ears?"

"They are hardly ornaments." The sergeant laughed. "They are police weapons, boy. When they are in place about the wrists of a prisoner, there is little he may do to escape."

"Oh, I see. Are they worn forever afterward?"

"Not at all. In each of them is a small lock. See, here is the key. When I open the lock, the handcuffs fall apart, like this, and the man is free to do as he wishes once more."

"How wonderful!" proclaimed Little Raven. "The white man is truly to be envied his fine brain. What weapons!" The boy paused a moment, brightening. "Red Coat," he asked, "if I were to go to the white man's school, would I learn about such remarkable things as these hahndcufts you show me?"

"I doubt it." The sergeant grinned. Then his words turned serious as quickly. "No, in school, boy, you are taught really remarkable and wonderful things. When a boy has been through school, they say he can capture men with words alone."

"I would rather have the hahndcufts," insisted Little Raven. "Those people in that school do not know Knife Eye!"

"Perhaps not." The sergeant nodded. "Yet, I want you

to remember our little talk. Go to school if your father should tell you to go. Do not argue and do not run away. Do I have your promise, Little Raven?"

The Mandan youth made the salute of the mounted police. "Yes, Red Coat," he said. "I will go to school if you order it. But now you must tell me something. Suppose Knife Eye does not surrender without fighting? Will you use the rifle upon him?"

"Not unless he forces me to do so."

"What if he begins shooting at us?"

"If he does that, I shall hide you carefully in some safe place and go after him."

"Without using the rifle?"

"Yes, if that is possible."

"But why should you risk your life, Red Coat? Knife Eye would shoot you without one moment's regret."

"I have a different oath to obey. The mounted police never use the rifle until the last thing. It is part of what you Indians would call our honor-word."

"Oh, I am sorry . . . I did not understand that." Little Raven made the respect sign, touching his fingertips to his forehead. "Nevertheless," he added stoutly, "you will need the rifle with Knife Eye. He is a bad Indian."

"We shall see. Better put the little dog back in your coat. We are going to travel again."

The Mandan youth did not object. He helped kick snow over the place where Sergeant Mackenzie knocked out the embers of the tobacco in his pipe. When the last small black flake was covered, with no wisp of blue smoke yet curling up, the big policeman led the way onward.

The wind was beginning to rise again. Strong as he was, the white man had to lean against the gale in order to make good progress on the snowshoes. However, his body offered fine shelter for Little Raven following in his footsteps, and the boy came along bravely behind him. As well, the snow-shoes of the first traveler always packed the trail for those who were second or third. Still it was hard going.

With the sun dropping swiftly now beyond the black shadows of the forest, the air grew colder. Little Raven's bones ached and he yearned to stop and build the fire for the night. But he was not ready to whimper. He wanted, above all, for the Red Coat to understand that he, too, was a good policeman.

At last, the sergeant stopped. Pointing ahead, he spoke in a low voice. "Do you see that narrow place where the frozen stream passes between those high steep banks?" he asked the Indian youth.

"I see it," answered Little Raven. "But we cannot camp there. The snow will drift and fill up that place during the night. We would be covered by the morning."

"Ah, but you have not noticed the large rock which juts out from the one bank. You see, that rock will hold up the drifting snow. It cannot bury us. The more it drifts over us during the night, the cozier we shall be like two bears and one small cub in a hibernation cave. Come on, Little Raven. I am tired."

"Oh, well," said the Indian boy, "if that is the case, then let us camp as you say. For myself, I could go on another ten miles, or more. Easily."

Sergeant Mackenzie stared at him a moment. "Excuse me," he said quietly, "I had not realized how selfish I was being. Go ahead, lead the way. We will keep going. Ten miles, did you say?"

"No, wait!" cried Little Raven, alarmed. "It is I who forget his courtesy rules. If you are weary, we must rest. I insist upon it."

"You're right, Little Raven," said the big man softly. "We must obey the courtesy rules."

They went forward toward the camping place, each watching the other for a sign of a smile. Little Raven and Red Coat were not precisely certain which one was fooling the other. Finally the Mandan lad nodded to himself. He was satisfied. When it came to craftiness with words, no white man could dream of deceiving any Indian.

When they reached the narrow deep banks, they put down their burdens under the rock. For the sergeant, it was the rolled-up scarlet blanket, his back pack, his short rifle, his pouch of ammunition. For the dark-skinned boy, it was the little puppy, Black Moccasin, and his own bone-weary body. Looking about him, Little Raven nodded. It was a wonderful spot in there under that large overhanging rock. It was safe and warm and dry, with no snow blowing into it. There was even some good firewood that had drifted up along the edges of the small stream.

"This is a fine camp, Red Coat," he admitted. "You are a real hunter. You have the eyes of a Mandan."

The policeman regarded him carefully. Little Raven could not be certain if he was smiling, or if his blue eyes always twinkled that way behind the sober look.

"And you, Little Raven," he said, "have the mind of a white man."

The Indian boy had it in his mind to inquire if this was good or bad, but he was not given the chance. As his friend Red Coat was leaning down to place the precious rifle in a protected place before building the night's fire, a quavery sound rose on the still air of the winter twilight. It was a sound that Little Raven knew well. So did Red Coat. Instinctively the Mandan youth reached down and picked up the wolf dog puppy.

172

"Timber wolves," said Sergeant Mackenzie quietly. "A large band of them."

"They have something surrounded," said the Indian youth. "That is their closing cry. Ah, the poor deer, the poor caribou, or moose calf. My heart weeps for you, whatever you are."

"Be still," ordered the police sergeant. "That's no deer or moose, and no caribou. Listen."

Little Raven bent his ear toward the sound.

"An old panther, perhaps? A weak or sickly bear?"

"No, listen harder."

The Indian boy did so, feeling his skin tingle strangely. "There's a snarling there which is not the snarling of wolves," he whispered. "Is that what you mean?"

"That's it," answered Sergeant Mackenzie. "Those are sled dogs! That's a *man* with a team of sled dogs the wolf pack has trapped over there . . . !"

Twenty-Six

On their snowshoes they ran swiftly through the woodland fringe toward the sound of the yelping pack. Sergeant Mackenzie had his carbine unslung. He called back to Little Raven to stay close by his heels, not to fall behind. In his own small hand, the Indian youth carried the rusted axe from Cheyenne Man's lodge. It was very still in the forest, as they ran. Frost smoke clouded from their lungs. The soft slapping of their webbed snowshoes kicked up plumes of powdery flakes. Within a short time they broke clear of the trees and saw the man and his team of dogs surrounded by the snarling wolves.

The latter had not yet made their closing rush. They were still circling nearer and nearer to the man and the brave dogs. The man stood with his rifle in his hands. The dogs were all tethered to the overturned sled so that they might not foolishly charge out at the wolves and so be killed, one by one. Little Raven peered ahead, thrilled as well as frightened by the terrible outcries and swift rushes of the wolves. Then, of a sudden, his dark eyes widened. He knew that man and those dogs!

"Red Coat!" he called excitedly. "That is Knife Eye who the wolves have trapped!"

Sergeant Mackenzie's words were stern and quick.

"Are you certain, boy?"

"Yes, yes, of course! I know the dogs. See that great black brute, there? The one wanting most to get at the wolves? That's yellow-eyed Chaka. That fierce devil. He fears nothing on this earth. *Hee-yahhh,* Chaka! It is I, Kagohami, the Little Raven! Do not despair . . . we will save you!"

The Mandan boy shouted the last words across the snowy stillness, his heart pounding. He did not know why he thus called out encouragement to the great black dog. Chaka was vicious and a certain killer. It was a sure thing that he would attack Little Raven in a moment were not the wolves and his tether keeping him from breaking free. Yet the great animal was so totally unafraid of the fearsome pack that the Indian youth could not help but admire him.

Sergeant Mackenzie, however, was not admiring Chaka. "You, Knife Eye!" he called in Mandan to the Assiniboin. "We will help you. Do not shoot at us. We are coming over there to join you against the wolves. Keep your dogs off of us when we come in!"

With a shout, and before Little Raven might imagine what was intended, the big Red Coat scooped him up and swung him across his broad shoulder like a sack of beans.

"Hang on tightly!" he called to the boy. "Here we go!"

His voice seemed merry; his blue eyes flashed. He ran straight across the open snow and straight at the circling wolf pack. The savage animals, hearing his shout and seeing him come at them, became confused. They hesitated, growling and snapping at one another, as wolves always do when surprised. Then their leader, an enormous tawny-bellied female, uttered a squalling yelp of rage and retreated toward the forest.

Some of the others tucked their bushy tails between their

legs and followed her. Their momentary cowardice opened up the circle of their pack mates about Knife Eye and the sled dogs. Through this opening, the Red Coat dashed swiftly. Almost before Little Raven could catch his breath, the policeman had reached the side of Knife Eye and the overturned sled. Setting the Mandan boy upon the ground behind the dogs, and behind the medicine man, he said sternly to Little Raven: "Do not move away from the sled. The dogs will guard you until the last." With that, he took two strides through the dogs and came up face-to-face with the Assiniboin.

The two tall men, one dark of skin, the other fair, stood staring at one another. It was a moment of deepest silence.

Out beyond Red Coat and Knife Eye, the wolf pack cowards were returning to join their braver mates once more. They made no sound and thus were even more frightening than when snarling loudly. The sled dogs, too, even great Chaka, had ceased their growling. Closer and closer circled the wolves. Little Raven felt his legs grow weak with fear. He took a firmer grasp upon his rusted camp axe. He glanced hopefully toward Sergeant Mackenzie. But the Red Coat was not watching Little Raven or the wolves. He was watching Knife Eye.

It was the medicine man who lost his nerve first. It was he who spoke the opening words.

"What lies has this boy told you?" he demanded of the blue-eyed policeman.

"No lies," answered the other. "Only the truth, and all of the truth."

"The truth about what?" challenged the medicine man.

"The truth about the whisky," said Sergeant Mackenzie, gambling that his words would startle the Assiniboin into admitting his guilt. "I shall have to arrest you, to put hand-

cuffs upon your wrists and take you to the prison at Fort Great Slave in my country."

"I was afraid of that." Knife Eye nodded, his face hardening.

"You have reason to be afraid of it," the sergeant told him. "It will be many years in the prison for you. Five winters at the least. Perhaps ten."

Knife Eye was no coward. At the harsh words, he only shrugged his heavy shoulders. He even smiled a small, hard smile. He was accepting his fate, like all Indians, with toughness and without making excuses.

"Well," he said, "a few years in your nice warm prison is better than being stripped of all my clothing and run naked into the snows by that old rascal, Black Cat, which is what the Mandans would do to me. *Bah!* That Black Cat! A great chief *he* is. He was my best customer!"

"So the boy told me," answered the sergeant calmly.

Little Raven, listening to the exchange, had taken his eyes from the wolves a moment. Now he looked back at them. His heart nearly stopped beating. The wolves had moved in so closely that the Indian boy could scent their rank odor on the wind. They were no more than the toss of a pebble away. Little Raven started to call out in warning to Sergeant Mackenzie.

But Knife Eye was there before him. *"Ai-hai,* Red Coat!" shouted the medicine man. "Watch that big gray wolf to your right." With the shout, Knife Eye fired his rifle not two feet from the mounted policeman's face. But the bullet did not touch Sergeant Mackenzie. It whistled past him and struck a huge, smoke-colored wolf that was in the act of springing at the policeman from the side. The wolf turned over in mid-air from the force of the bullet. It fell into the snow with a dreadful whimper, and lay still where it fell.

"Good shooting!" called back the sergeant to Knife Eye. "And you might do well to watch that big, dark female to your left there!" Then he shot at the wolf that was trying to sneak in behind Knife Eye and come at the sled. At the shot, the dark female dropped as limply as had the gray male to the bullet of Knife Eye.

"Thank you," was all that the medicine man said to his companion. But Little Raven was sure that he saw a look of gratitude on the Assiniboin's fierce face. This fact increased his own confidence in the fight.

"Good shooting to both of you!" he cried out to the two tall riflemen.

He had thought to be cheerful and to show braveness, but Sergeant Mackenzie wheeled about swiftly. His face was not cheerful nor was it smiling in any way.

"Be quiet," he ordered in a low voice. "Hold your axe ready at all times. If any of the wolves sneak in behind Knife Eye and myself, you must strike at them with the blade, as you call your warning. Let them know your arm, even if small, has sharp steel in the end of it."

As he spoke to Little Raven, he yelled loudly and kicked a great cloud of snow at the wolves. The animals drew back surprised and snarling.

"Get behind the dogs!" the sergeant shouted at Knife Eye. "You and I will stand back-to-back, with the boy between us. Hurry up now!"

Knife Eye did not argue. He obeyed the command quickly.

"Little Raven," the sergeant called sternly, "you stay with the dogs, no matter what happens to Knife Eye and myself! Keep close to the Chaka dog. Do you hear me?"

"Yes, all right, I hear you, Red Coat!"

The Mandan boy leaped to place himself at great

Chaka's side. The black brute snarled at him, then, strangely, he wagged his tail and whined. Little Raven ignored him for the moment. He was worrying about the words of the Red Coat.

The policeman was thinking that, even if he and Knife Eye were to be pulled down by a charge of the wolf pack, some of the wolves would be shot in the affair. Perhaps enough of them so that the hardy sled dogs, led by Chaka, might protect the small Indian lad successfully from the remaining wolves. Little Raven understood that and was grateful for it, but it made him very fearful. Nor was the fear unreasonable.

The twilight was nearly gone, giving away to the true night. The slanted eyes of the wolves glowed in the deepening gloom. Their red tongues panted rapidly. Their white teeth gleamed and champed.

Without warning, one of them darted inward toward the sled. Another wolf followed the first. A third leaped after the second. A fourth and fifth howled wildly and dashed in from the opposite direction. On the instant, it seemed to Little Raven, wolves were everywhere. Knife Eye and the Red Coat stood like giants, working their rifles with incredible speed of reloading and firing. Their bullets smashed down wolf after wolf. The animals were writhing in mid-air, in the snow, crawling away, lying unconscious, yelping in the agony of their wounds, or silent with the stillness of the dead. Still the others of the pack came on.

"Get beneath the sled!" shouted the sergeant to Little Raven.

The Indian youth dug into the snow, burying himself under the overturned sled. Chaka, seeing him do this, leaped to stand guard over him, just as two wolves attempted to rush in and seize the boy. The wolves drew away, afraid to close with the black sled dog.

Now came a moment when, halted by the rifle fire of the two men and given pause by the fierce lungings of the sled dogs, it seemed that the pack would give way and flee. It was at this very instant that Sergeant Mackenzie, turning to aim at one of the hesitant brutes, twisted his ankle and fell heavily into the snow.

To the pack this was a signal to attack, not retreat. A wolf will forget all caution when he sees his victim falter and go down. Nothing would stop a pack that senses its moment of the kill has arrived. In the present case, the gray phantoms wheeled about and came raging back in to finish off the fallen policeman.

The medicine man, Knife Eye, did not move to help his comrade of the moment before. Evidently his rifle was unloaded or jammed so that it would not fire. In terror, Little Raven realized there was nothing remaining between the mounted policeman and certain death except—he and his rusted chopping axe. Yet, even as the fear of this came to the small Mandan, he uttered a shrill Indian cry and charged the wolves.

The brutes were so completely startled to see one tiny, dark-skinned human rush at them in this fashion that they gave ground long enough for Little Raven to reach the side of the Red Coat. He thought, then, that the policeman would recover and arise. But the latter did not arise. It was then that the Indian lad understood that his tall friend must have struck his head upon the hard ice of the ground in falling, rendering himself senseless for the moment.

"Help us!" the boy cried out to Knife Eye. "Help the Red Coat as he helped you!"

His only reply from the gaunt medicine man was an ugly laugh that was echoed by a snarling of the wolf pack.

"Save the Red Coat yourself!" the Assiniboin shouted, using a pause during which the wolves were re-gathering to come in once more on the helpless policeman. "I have eight more rifle shells here, and there are but seven wolves remaining. Hah! Do you think I any longer need you and that cursed Red Coat? May the Dark One receive you both. Especially you, you sneaking Mandan half-breed mongrel, you! Have a good journey to the Land of the Shadows, boy! You've earned it. When you get up there, tell the gods that the Assiniboin whisky seller sent you! Farewell, Red Coat. Farewell, little spy. *Bah . . . !*"

Before Little Raven, coming out of the darkening shade of the forest trees, loomed the hairy forms of the great wolves. Their eyes were flames of green fire. He could feel the hot splash of their slobber strike his face and his hands. The stink of their fetid breaths fouled his cheeks, stung his nostrils. There was no time to pray.

Twenty-Seven

In that final moment, when the wolves closed in upon Little Raven, help came from the gods all the same. The voice that called for that help was not Little Raven's. It was the tiny, high-pitched yapping of the wolf dog puppy, Black Moccasin. The small beast had been forgotten in the swift danger of the fight at the sled. But he was still nestled inside Little Raven's wolf-skin coat, and, when the strong odor of the wolf smell struck his young nose, he uttered his shrill yelp of terror and alarm.

The cry was answered by such a deep-throated roaring snarl as Little Raven had never heard. It came from the direction of the sled, and it came from the chest of the black lead dog, Chaka. With the enraged roar, Chaka burst his tether with one mighty lunge. He flew at the wolves closing in upon Little Raven and Black Moccasin. But all in an instant the savage pack had stormed him under, and the Indian boy saw the valiant lead dog disappear beneath the mass of wolf bodies. The sound that the wolves made, as they surged over Chaka, chilled the blood of Little Raven. The sound also froze his limbs with fear. He could not lift his feet to run for his camp axe to help Chaka.

While he stood there, helplessly, other aid came for the brave lead dog. It came from his master, Knife Eye. The

182

medicine man did not want to lose his great team leader. He would need him in any possible flight to escape from the unconscious Red Coat. So Knife Eye rushed in with his rifle, trying for a shot at some of the wolves, a shot that would not injure Chaka. He could find no such shot. As he stood there, cursing his anger in the Assiniboin tongue, the big Red Coat sergeant recovered his senses.

The policeman staggered to his feet, shaking his bruised head. He saw the wolves on Chaka. Without thinking, he used his short rifle as a steel club, swinging it by the barrel. He fell upon the wolves with an anger Little Raven would not have dreamed lay in such a friendly, smiling man.

One wolf he struck across the ribs with the iron-shod butt of the carbine. The wolf cried out in mortal hurt and dragged itself aside to lay thrashing in the red snow. He smashed a second wolf over the head with the old gun, breaking the bones of the skull. A third wolf quit the lead dog and ran for its life. The last one of the four wolves that had leaped upon the dog was too slow in its retreat, however. The heavy carbine's stock hit the creature in mid-spine, making it cry out as if torn in two pieces. It dragged itself to the nearby trees, where its vicious comrades fell upon it and destroyed it in a moment.

The fight was over, but the victory had been a dear one. Brave Chaka lay on his side in the snow. The crimson of his blood stained the white flakes all about him. Little Raven was certain that the poor fellow was dying and that he and the great dog would next meet in the Land of the Shadows. But Sergeant Mackenzie knew about more things than making wounds. He knew, also, how to heal them.

At once he set to work to save the life of Chaka. When he had the injuries bandaged and securely tied with thongs of soft buckskin from his back pack, he lifted the big dog in his arms and carried him to the sled. Righting the vehicle with Little Raven's help, he placed the wounded animal gently upon the riding furs of Knife Eye. Chaka's amber-yellow eyes stared up at the Red Coat.

"Lie quietly," said the policeman. "You are going to ride in the sled for a change and your master is going to help pull you."

He turned to look for Knife Eye, but he was too late. The treacherous Assiniboin, taking advantage of the tense work over the wounded Chaka, had stolen up behind Sergeant Mackenzie. He had the long black rifle pointed squarely at him. The muzzle was not one foot from the face of the tall policeman. Sergeant Mackenzie had laid aside his own rifle to care for the dog. He was helpless.

"Do not move," said Knife Eye in his deep voice, "or I shall blow away your head."

The mounted policeman showed no fear. "Think carefully what you are doing," he answered Knife Eye. "There are many Red Coats but only one of you. If you kill me, the Red Coats will hunt you down like a crazy beast of the forest. It is one thing to sell whisky. Do not think that killing a person is the same."

Knife Eye laughed his ugly laugh. "What care I for killing?" he sneered. "Do you think you are the first one I have shot? Hah! Ask this miserable Mandan boy here. Ask him what became of his Mandan warriors who tried to go for help to the Red Coats who live beyond Turtle Mountain. Ask him about Hard Shield and Two Elk. Go ahead, Red Coat, ask him."

Sergeant Mackenzie nodded. His voice was still calm. "What about Hard Shield and Two Elk, Little Raven?" he asked. "What happened to them?"

"They disappeared on the trail to Turtle Mountain," replied the frightened boy. "They never came back."

"They never will come back, either," said Knife Eye, glaring angrily. "I killed them both with this black gun of mine. One shot for each. Squarely between the shoulders. *Ih!* They died like dogs."

Sergeant Mackenzie's blue eyes looked straight into the cold face of Knife Eye. "If that is true," he said, "you will not go to prison."

"No?" exclaimed the medicine man, surprised.

"No," answered the mounted policeman. "You will be hanged by your neck."

Little Raven saw the Assiniboin whisky seller turn pale beneath his dark skin.

Knife Eye was very afraid, yet he recovered quickly. *"Bah!"* he snapped. "Your bones will be picked by the rest of those skulking wolves there in the forest. Your bones and the bones of this sneaking mixed-blood boy from the Mandan village. No one will ever know how you died. No bullets will be found. Only your bones, with the wolf tracks all around them."

Sergeant Mackenzie nodded. "If you are through talking with your big words," he said, "I will put the handcuffs on you and we will start out."

"One step toward me and I pull the trigger!" warned Knife Eye.

"You will pull it anyway when you are ready," said the policeman. "But fortunately it has taken you too long to get ready." The two men stood motionless for the space of one breath. Then the big sergeant nodded once more.

"Go ahead, Little Raven," he said.

Knife Eye cast a wild glance around for the Mandan boy. Too late he realized that the youth had disappeared. But Little Raven did not keep him waiting for the answer to where he had gone. For where he had gone was sneaking behind the sled and the black form of Chaka, to get behind the medicine man. And now, as Knife Eye hesitated in the moment's bewilderment, the lad brought down the blunt face of the chopping axe. He brought it down with a lusty swing at the same target it had struck two times before—the big toe of Knife Eye's large right foot.

The Assiniboin screeched and dropped his black rifle, seizing the wounded toe in its place. Sergeant Mackenzie leaped at once, his square fist doubled up hard as a rawhide hammer. He struck the medicine man a single blow only, but Little Raven heard the crunch of that single blow landing on Knife Eye's nose.

The gaunt Assiniboin went to his knees, blinded and dazed by the force of the policeman's brawny fist. Before his eyes recovered their normal vision, Sergeant Mackenzie had snapped the handcuffs upon his wrists and Knife Eye was the prisoner of the Red Coat from the Land of the Grandmother.

"Praise the gods," said Little Raven reverently. Then, after a pause, he added thoughtfully: "And also Sergeant Mackenzie."

Twenty-Eight

When Knife Eye's head had cleared and his knees were no longer wobbling from Sergeant Mackenzie's blow, the big policeman kept his promise to Chaka. He led the medicine man up to the front of the re-harnessed dog team and hitched him there in Chaka's place. Knife Eye complained bitterly but to no avail. Even Little Raven took his side, saying that it was a disgrace to the spirit for an Indian to do the work of sled dogs. Sergeant Mackenzie only smiled.

"Listen," he told the Indian boy, "this is the easiest way for me to watch my prisoner. After the way he turned on me just now, do you think I want him behind me again? No thank you. Indian spirit or no Indian spirit, he stays out there in front of the sled where I can see him all the while." The tall policeman lost his smile. "You were right about this fellow," he said, pointing to Knife Eye. "He *is* a bad Indian, a very bad one. But by the time he has helped pull this sled the rest of the way to your village, he will feel a lot less like fighting and shooting." He paused, looking about to see if everything was in readiness for the final departure. "Now, then," he concluded, "have we forgotten anything?"

As if in reply to his question, and before Little Raven himself might answer, the wolf dog puppy in his arms looked at the sergeant and barked yappingly.

187

At once the big man laughed. "Of course!" he called out delightedly. "I had forgotten you, little beauty! Bring him here, Little Raven. I want to show you something. Perhaps then you will understand why Chaka attacked the wolves as you told me."

The Mandan lad gave the puppy to the policeman. The latter threw back the Hudson's Bay blanket with which he had covered Chaka and held the little puppy down by the big dog's head. Chaka immediately showed great interest, nosing and sniffing at the tiny youngster almost as a mother might.

"Do you see that?" asked Sergeant Mackenzie. "Now, look carefully and you will see something else, I am sure."

Little Raven, peering at the big lead dog and the small black puppy, started to shake his head in puzzlement. Then a bright light of recognition spread over his dark face.

"Of course!" he cried. "I see it now! Oh, how blind I have been! *Ih!* They both have the same curly black hair like that of the bull buffalo, the same four white paws, the same large white star on the chest." He paused, staring up at the tall policeman, hope shining from his eyes. "Could it be possible, Red Coat?" he asked. "Could any mixed-blood Mandan boy be so fortunate?"

"You have guessed it." The sergeant grinned, putting the puppy in the sled with Chaka. "This little orphan wolf dog is an orphan no longer. He's Chaka's son."

With the announcement, he put the blanket back over the wounded lead dog and the puppy.

"*Now,*" he said again to Little Raven, "is there anything else we have forgotten?"

The Indian boy peeked beneath the blanket. He saw Black Moccasin nestled between the forepaws of his father, already fast asleep. He saw the look of pride that shone from Chaka's yellow eyes. He straightened, saluting Sergeant Mackenzie.

"Nothing else, Red Coat," he said. "We are ready."

Sergeant Mackenzie nodded, and picked up the small Mandan boy, swinging him into the sled beside Chaka and Black Moccasin.

"All right." He smiled. "Here we go. You ride with your friends. I'll follow along behind and do the driving from there."

With that, he uncurled the dog whip and sent its lash flicking out to bite at the rear-end of Knife Eye. The medicine man cursed him and glared blackly at him, but nevertheless settled into his harness and pulled ahead. His five sled dogs also leaped forward, eager to follow their captured master. The sled bounded along lightly as a feather from the flight wing of the hawk. Sergeant Mackenzie followed it on his snowshoes, his short rifle ready for any nonsense from Knife Eye. In the sled, Little Raven snuggled beneath the bright red Hudson's Bay blanket, his arms about his two fine black dogs. Soon he, too, was fast asleep. His dreams were the finest ones he ever had.

Twenty-Nine

They came to the Missouri River near the village of Little Raven in the full dark of the night. Sergeant Mackenzie ordered the sled halted in the willow brush of the riverbank, saying they would not go on into the village. "We shall leave Knife Eye here in the trees," he told Little Raven. "You can take me on into the caverns beneath his lodge, yonder there on the rocky point. After we have found the furs and the whisky that you say are there, then I shall tell you how it will be after that. I mean in regard to my prisoner and your village."

"But, Red Coat," objected the sleepy boy, "why do we stop here? Are you afraid of my people?"

"In a way, yes," admitted the big policeman. "You see, Little Raven, what I fear is that, when your people have heard the story of how Knife Eye has used them . . . cheating them out of their valuable furs with his evil whisky . . . having corn and meat to eat when they had none . . . lying to them to get their last half dozen fine ponies for his own . . . when they hear all of this, then I am afraid they will try to take my prisoner away from me."

"But why would they do that, Red Coat?"

"To give him a Mandan trial. To bring him to Indian justice."

"Is that a wrong thing?" asked Little Raven, awake now and beginning to worry. "If you let my people have Knife Eye, then you will not have to worry about taking him all that way back up to the Land of the Grandmother."

"That is just the trouble, boy. The Mandans would kill him without a fair trial. They would strip him naked and drive him out into the snow to freeze to death."

"But he deserves it, Red Coat!"

"Perhaps. But first he deserves a fair trial. That is part of my honor-word as a Red Coat . . . to see that every prisoner is brought safely in and given a fair trial for his crime, whatever it may be."

"Even if he has killed?"

"Yes, boy, even if he has killed."

Little Raven shook his head, very puzzled by this. "The white man has strange laws," he said. "The Indian way is better. It is much quicker."

"Quicker and better are not the same, lad," said the big policeman gravely. "Slow and sure is the way the white man's justice works."

"But . . . ," the Indian boy began again.

"No more buts," ordered Sergeant Mackenzie. "We will not argue law out here in this cold, eh? We have a lot to do yet. Besides, small Indian friend, in this case I *am* the law and you will obey me. Is that a true thing?"

"Yes," said Little Raven, saluting him. "I believe it is."

"Good." His companion smiled. "Remember, now, we must be quiet and quick in this matter. Your people may still be out looking for you, or wondering where Knife Eye has gone. So we must hurry. But we must make no noise."

He turned away from Little Raven to the medicine man. Taking the latter out of the dog harness, he handcuffed him to one of the willow trees.

Will Henry

"There," he nodded to Knife Eye. "Unless you pull up that tree by the roots, you will still be there when I return for you. As for keeping quiet, I know I can trust you. Unless, of course, you prefer Mandan justice to white man's law."

"You may trust me," growled the Assiniboin. "Those Mandan devils owe me a little too much. Besides, you have not gotten me back up in Canada just yet. It is a long journey and many things can happen along its lonely path."

"Nothing will happen," said the red-coated sergeant.

Knife Eye shook his head. He lifted his upper lips, showing his teeth. Little Raven could not say if it was meant to be a sneer or a smile.

"Do not be so certain," said the medicine man. "Remember Two Elk and Hard Shield. They also planned to make the long journey to Turtle Mountain without my permission."

"I'm not forgetting them or what happened to them."

"*Bah,* you'll never find their bones."

"Perhaps not. But in my mind I know what you did to them, and I know why you did it."

At this point, Little Raven came forward. "I could never imagine why anyone would want to harm Two Elk and Hard Shield," he said to the sergeant. "Knife Eye has boasted to you that he shot them in the back with his rifle. But why did he do that? Did he want the Mandans to starve? That does not seem sensible, Red Coat. Then he would have no one remaining to sell his whisky to. Am I right?"

"You are right, and you are not right," said the big policeman. "You see, the most important thing to this bad Indian was that no news must be allowed to reach the Red Coats concerning him. Knife Eye was known to us. He had

192

a bad name in Canada, too. As I have said, he was a Canadian Indian. He knew that, if we found out where he was, that we would come after him for the other crimes he was accused of in our own land. Had we come here and heard of him selling whisky to American Indians, it would only have gone the harder for him. He knew that, Little Raven. That's why he would kill to keep Two Elk and Hard Shield from getting to Turtle Mountain. That's what your wise new father, Cheyenne Man, also knew about Knife Eye. That is, he knew that Knife Eye was the one who had 'used his magic' to keep those two brave Mandans from reaching the Red Coat police. That is also why your father told you that only the Red Coats might save the Mandans."

"I still say," growled Knife Eye, interrupting, "just what I said in the beginning. The way to Turtle Mountain is a long journey and many things can happen upon that lonely path."

Sergeant Mackenzie stepped back close to his prisoner. "You know very well how long that journey is, Knife Eye," he told him, low-voiced. "For you are going to make every step of it just as you made the journey here tonight . . . pulling the sled with your five dogs. And I will tell you more. You will also pull upon that sled the evidence which will bring the white man's justice upon you. You will carry your own doom with you, and you deserve to do so."

Knife Eye did not reply to this.

The last that Little Raven saw of him, the Assiniboin medicine man was glaring at him and at Sergeant Mackenzie, his eyes full of the final fright of a trapped animal.

The Mandan boy turned away with a shiver. He went to the front of the sled and took Sergeant Mackenzie's big hand.

"Come on, Red Coat," he said. "Here is your friend,

Little Raven, to help you find the whisky and the furs."

"Thank you, Little Raven," said the policeman soberly, and called softly to the sled dogs to—"Mush!"—meaning for them to start out and pull the sled before the Mandan boy and himself. As the dogs obeyed, the boy fell into step beside the big sergeant.

Looking up at him, he nodded with great dignity. "You don't need to thank me, Red Coat," he said. "In this hard life, one good policeman must help another."

They went on to the river cavern entrance, saying no more.

At the caverns, the work was hard but brief. Sergeant Mackenzie loaded up the sled with whisky jugs he opened and poured out on the cavern's floor, so the Mandans would not be tempted to drink any of the evil stuff. He took with him, as well, a little of the dried meat and corn to feed the prisoner, the sled dogs, and himself.

The remainder of the corn and the meat, and all of the beautiful furs, he left for the Mandan people. There was food enough, he told Little Raven, to restore the people's strength so that they might travel to Turtle Mountain with their furs and trade for more food to see them through the entire winter in safety and good health. The people could thank Little Raven for this gift of the gods, the big policeman added.

Then it became very quiet between the small Mandan boy and himself, for both of them knew that the time had come to say good bye. Sergeant Mackenzie took the hand of Little Raven in his own hand, as if they were men of equal years.

"Little Raven," he said, "always be honorable and brave. Serve your people well when you are chief one day. Think often of your friend, Red Coat. Remember to obey your father and go to the white man's school when you are able. Take good care of big Chaka and little Black Moccasin. In the way that the trails of red and white men take their separate paths, we shall not likely see one another again. Let us say farewell and good hunting, Kagohami."

When he used Little Raven's Mandan name, the boy stood straight as a young pine tree.

"I will give you my honor-word on all of these things, Red Coat," he replied. "Through all of my winters I will remember you. I will always try to do my best for you."

The silence came between them once more, then. They looked at one another, each wanting to say more. Neither could do it, however.

Sergeant Mackenzie turned away to take up his short rifle and the dog whip. He spoke to the sled dogs. They whined and began to pull. The sled started away. Little Raven could not stand that, and he ran after the sled. The big policeman stopped the dogs and waited for him.

When the Mandan boy had run up to him, he picked him up in his strong arms. He gave him a bear hug and a kiss on the cheek. He tasted the salt of tears and knew that the Indian lad was weeping. He said nothing, and the boy hugged him and gave him a shy kiss in return. When he put the small youth down again, no words were required. Red Coat and Little Raven had said good bye with their hearts.

Thirty

~

Little Raven, with Chaka limping by his side and with Black Moccasin again hidden in his wolf-skin coat, went on through the night toward the village. He knew that Black Cat, the chief, was not going to be pleased to be awakened at this late hour. Older people did not like to get up at night. Besides, it was snowing hard once more and growing very cold again.

Nonetheless, the boy entered the sleeping village and hurried to the chief's lodge. There, he stood outside the entrance way, calling the name of Black Cat.

"Come out, come out, my chief!" he cried. "It is I, Little Raven, come back safely and with important news!"

Black Cat, when he finally poked his wrinkled face into the snowy night, was not pleased. "Fool boy!" he snapped. "What do you think you are doing standing out there shouting my name at this hour? Wait a moment . . . I will get my dog whip and give you a lashing. *Ih!* Can't a man even starve in peace?"

Little Raven moved more closely in toward the fire's light falling upon the opened entry skins. "But you don't have to starve any more, my chief," he explained. "That is what I have come to tell you. I know where there is plenty of good food, both meat and corn. We have been saved by the Red Coat police!"

"Eh? What is that? Food? Saved? Red Coats? You lie, you young whelp! Where is that whip of mine?"

But Little Raven pushed past the old man, into the lodge. There he told his entire story, but did not receive the blessing he had expected.

"Do you think I'm crazy?" asked Black Cat. "Such a wild tale of great wolf packs? Of a Red Coat policeman as tall as a pine tree? Of you striking Knife Eye three times with that old hatchet? Of all our furs and much food stored in magic river caves beneath the lodge of the medicine man?"

"But, my chief," pleaded the boy, "at least permit me to show you where the food is. Are you not hungry? Would you not like some fat meat and boiled corn?"

This was too much for the old man. He began to lick his lips. Fetching his buffalo robe, he wound it about him. "Lead the way, boy," he growled. "But if you are lying and Knife Eye curses us with some evil spell, it will go very hard with you."

"Knife Eye is gone away to prison. The Red Coat has taken him in the hahndcufts. We will never see that medicine man again in our lifetimes."

"*Bah!* Keep going and be quiet."

But it was too late to be quiet. The old man had been talking very loud and the villagers were beginning to awaken. Heads came poking out of other lodges. Soon several of the Mandan people were following along the street with the chief and Little Raven, all asking for the boy's story. He repeated it for them. Some of them laughed. Some of them grew afraid to go on to Knife Eye's lodge. None of them believed the boy.

When the party came to the rocky point and the taboo

ground of the medicine man's lodge, Black Cat held up his hand. He and the boy would enter alone, he said. This would lessen the anger of Knife Eye, should the Assiniboin prove to be at home.

But the Assiniboin was not at home. In a few moments the old chief came back out of the lodge, his eyes wide with disbelief.

"Come into this house of evil!" he cried. "See for yourselves what Little Raven has found here!"

The Mandans went into the lodge. They brought out the meat and the corn and the furs, then they released the seven ponies and led them outside. The ponies were returned to their masters. The dried meat and the corn were divided equally among the people. As the Red Coat had promised, there was enough meat to feed them all until they could go to Turtle Mountain with the furs and trade for supplies that would take them through the entire winter. There was even corn enough to feed the ponies until their owners regained their strength and might once more go into the forest and cut willow bark and boughs for them to eat. It was a wonderful moment for them all. Even Black Cat was gracious. When Cheyenne Man came up from the village just as the last of the things were being carried from Knife Eye's lodge, the chief made a speech, waiting only until Cheyenne Man had embraced his adopted son and made certain the boy was well.

"My people," announced Black Cat, "we owe this food and the return of our furs to Little Raven. He has shown a brave heart. Although he has sought to garnish his tale with some extra adventures of Red Coat police and handcuffs and fights with wolf packs in the forest, we surely forgive him these small lies. The important thing is that he told the truth about Knife Eye and led us to these precious treasures here, which will save all of our lives."

Little Raven tried to interrupt, to insist that he told no lies, that he could show them the tracks of the Red Coat in the snow by the riverbank. But it was useless to attempt stopping a Mandan chief who has begun a big speech. Ignoring the boy, Black Cat swept on.

"Now," he said, "one way or another, Little Raven has driven Knife Eye away. He is gone, and five of his six dogs are gone, and here is Little Raven with the black lead dog, Chaka, to show us he has the victory. So now by Indian law all the belongings that were Knife Eye's go to this boy."

The people applauded this fact, but Little Raven was still trying to explain that he did not lie about the Red Coat.

"Be still, foolish boy," chided Cheyenne Man. "Knife Eye had many fine things. You will be rich."

But the boy would not be still, so the tribe went down to the river's bank and looked for the tracks of the Red Coat in the snow. Alas, the new snow had already fallen deeply. There were no tracks of anything showing down at the river's bank. The people came back up to the lodge of Knife Eye, believing the Red Coat to be nothing more than an imagination of Little Raven's mind. Still, they accepted his defeat of Knife Eye, even if they could not explain it.

They hoisted the boy on their shoulders and returned him to the village in triumph. After the belongings of the medicine man were removed from the taboo lodge and given over to Little Raven, the lodge itself was burned to the ground, so that its evil would vanish with its owner.

All should have been happiness for Little Raven, yet it was not. His great tall friend, Red Coat, had left him with no evidence to prove his story.

In the end, the Indian's idea of law was really no different than the white man's: They were not willing to be-

lieve a thing without some article of hard evidence to show
that thing was true.

Cheyenne Man did his best to brighten the days for the
boy. But the long winter drew to its close without Little
Raven returning to his former good cheer and brave spirit.
The days of spring, with their warm sun, came to the land
of the Mandans. Soon it was time to leave the winter lodges
of the village and set forth for the summer buffalo hunting
upon the open plains to the west. The boy, who had been
praying all the while that the Red Coat would remember
him and would send him some evidence to show the people,
now gave up the last hope.

Red Coat had forgotten him. The big man with the
yellow hair and blue eyes had deserted his small dark friend,
Little Raven.

Yet on the final hour of the final day of the leaving for
the buffalo pastures, when all the ponies were saddled and
all the riders mounted, there came a great shout from the
north. All eyes turned to the riverbank trail to Turtle
Mountain. Coming down that trail upon a spotted horse
that flew fleet as the wind was a Canadian Sioux Indian.

All of the tribe knew him. He was the rider who carried
the white man's mail between Turtle Mountain and the
Land of the Grandmother.

The band drew in its ponies and waited, wondering with
excitement what brought the Canadian mail rider so far
south, and at such a fast pace.

The rider did not keep them wondering for long. Sliding
his beautiful mount to a halt, he called out to Black Cat, the
chief.

"Ho, there, Black Cat! Is there one among your band
who calls himself Kagohami, the Little Raven?"

Black Cat pointed out the boy, while the Mandans got off their ponies and crowded about to see what was to come.

The mail rider saluted Little Raven. As he did this, some of the Mandans laughed.

The Sioux horsemen stared haughtily at them.

"Here," he said to Little Raven, taking a flat, square package from his saddlebags. "Open this and show these yapping prairie coyotes how simple they are in their minds."

The boy took the packet and removed its wrappings. What was revealed within when he did so brought a gasp from all of the Mandans. It was a small red coat of the brightest scarlet, cut especially to fit Little Raven and designed precisely like the famous coats of the Northwest Mounted Police.

Nor was this all. Upon each sleeve were three chevron stripes, the same as those upon the coat of Sergeant Mackenzie, and upon the breast, embroidered on a shield of beadwork, were these words in the white man's tongue:

TO SERGEANT LITTLE RAVEN
From his friends
of the Red Coat
Police

Nor was this all, even yet. The mail rider had another package for the Mandan boy. This second package was narrow and flat and heavy. In it was the long black rifle of Knife Eye. Of course, there could be no pride greater than that.

Black Cat himself helped Little Raven into the red coat. The chief then lifted the boy up on his beautiful buffalo horse, while he walked beside the animal. Behind them came Cheyenne Man on his gray racer, Bright Arrow, carrying the long black rifle for his brave son. Following them came the other Mandans, each riding or leading the new ponies that they had been able to buy that spring with the money from their furs. All of the people were happy. All of them were well.

Little Raven felt the warm sunshine on his face. In his arms he carried the wolf dog puppy, Black Moccasin. By the side of his horse paced the great lead dog, Chaka, yellow eyes upturned to watch his new small master.

The three friends led the Mandan village that day, as it set out toward the buffalo pastures. No Indian boy of but eleven winters was ever granted higher honor than that in the land of the Mandans.

About the Author

Henry Wilson Allen wrote under both the Clay Fisher and Will Henry bylines and was a five-time winner of the Spur Award from the Western Writers of America. He was born in Kansas City, Missouri. His early work was in short subject departments with various Hollywood studios, and he was working at M-G-M when his first Western novel, *No Survivors* (1950), was published. While numerous Western authors before Allen provided sympathetic and intelligent portraits of Indian characters, Allen from the start set out to characterize Indians in such a way as to make their viewpoints an integral part of his stories. *Red Blizzard* (1951) was his first Western novel under the Clay Fisher byline and remains one of his best. Some of Allen's images of Indians are of the romantic variety, to be sure, but his theme often is the failure of the American frontier experience and the romance is used to treat his tragic themes with sympathy and humanity. On the whole, the Will Henry novels tend to be based more deeply in actual historical events, whereas in the Clay Fisher titles he was more intent on a story filled with action that moves rapidly. However, this dichotomy can be misleading, since *MacKenna's Gold* (1963), a Will Henry Western about gold-seekers, reads much as one of the finest Clay Fisher titles, *The Tall Men* (1954).

His novels, *I, Tom Horn* (1975), *One More River to Cross* (1967), *Journey to Shiloh* (1960), *Chiricahua* (1972), and *From Where the Sun Now Stands* (1960) in particular, remain imperishable classics of Western historical fiction. Over a dozen films have been made based on his work.

"I am but a solitary horseman of the plains, born a century too late and far away," Allen once wrote about himself. He felt out of joint with his time, and what alone may ultimately unify his work is the vividness of his imagination, the tremendous emotion with which he invested his characters and fashioned his Western stories. At his best, he wove an almost incomparable spell that involves a reader deeply in his narratives, informed always by his profound empathy for so many of the casualties of the historical process. *The Hunkpapa Scout* will be his next **Five Star Western.**

The employees of Five Star hope you have enjoyed this book. All our books are made to last. Other Five Star books are available at your library, through selected bookstores, or directly from us.

For information about titles, please call:

(800) 223-1244

or visit our Web site at:

www.gale.com/fivestar

To share your comments, please write:

Publisher
Five Star
295 Kennedy Memorial Drive
Waterville, ME 04901